THE THIRD
CORONA BOOK OF
HORROR
STORIES

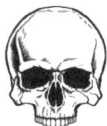

THE THIRD CORONA BOOK OF
HORROR STORIES

edited by
LEWIS WILLIAMS

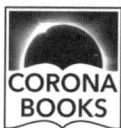

CORONA BOOKS

First published in the United Kingdom in 2019
1

by Corona Books UK
www.coronabooks.com

ISBN 978-1-9996579-4-9

Cover design by Martin Bushell
www.creatusadvertising.co.uk

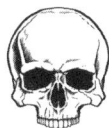

CONTENTS

Editor's Introduction   7

Suds and Monsters *by Christopher Stanley*   11
The Debt *by John Haas*   17
Old Gods *by Sue Bentley*   45
Curious, If Anything *by C.C. Adams*   57
Cancer the Crab *by Lewis Williams*   68
Worse Things *by Molly Thynes*   70
Believe and Be Justified *by Felix Flynn*   87
The Haunting of April Heights *by Tricia Lowther*   97
Angel *by Jo Gilmour*   110
Murderabilia *by Adam Meyer*   114
The First Circle *by Sue Eaton*   132
The Barber *by A.P. Sessler*   139
Luna Too *by Jess Doyle*   144
Roxy *by Viktoria Faust*   152
A Little Death *by Ryan Harville*   159
Gamer *by Richard A. Shury*   173
Cecily *by Colette Bennett*   178

Lily's Kids *by Florence Ann Marlowe*   189
Scythe *by Jeremy Megargee*   209

Author biographies   213
List of author websites and Twitter accounts   221
List of honourable mentions   223

INTRODUCTION

We were overwhelmed. We expected a great response to our open call for submissions for this book, but nothing prepared us for the 824 horror short story submissions we received, totalling over three million words! I kid you not, and we read them all.

So, first and foremost huge thanks go out to everyone who submitted stories for this book whether their stories were chosen or not. We received far more great stories than we had room for in the book. I know I've said it before, but there's so much horror writing talent out there that mainstream publishers are apt to ignore. We, on the other hand, have certainly gone the extra mile ourselves this time to take the time and trouble to seek out and celebrate the genuinely brilliant horror writing talent that is out there. Some of the authors with stories published in this book have had many past successes; others have had only little or none of their work published before. We simply chose the best of the stories we were submitted without fear or favour but with a lot of hard work, which brings me to my second debt of huge thanks…

That debt is to my fellow members of the selection panel – you know who you are. I think all of us spent virtually every free minute we had over the past few months reading the submissions, sometimes well into the small hours. (Perhaps that's the best time to read horror stories anyway.) And then after that, we faced some truly difficult decisions to arrive at a final selection for this book, which obviously couldn't include three million words and, in truth, could only contain about 2% of the material we received.

At one point we toyed with the idea of doubling that amount by doing *The Fourth Corona Book of Horror Stories* at the same time as this book and publishing both on the same day, in the same way Bruce Springsteen had so much material he wanted to get out there that he released two albums on the same day back in the 1990s! As it turned out, we've done something slightly different. This book *does* have a sister volume, *The Corona Book of Ghost Stories*, which is a project that had been at the back of our minds for some time but that we were able to make a reality with the help of others of the submissions we received for this book, those of an exclusively ghostly persuasion.

That still left us plenty of stories we would have been honoured to publish here had there been space for them, and at the end of the book you'll find our list of honourable mentions – a list of authors who submitted great stories that we long-listed for inclusion.

As I say, we had to make some difficult decisions – some very, very difficult decisions – and our final choices were shaped by bringing you the best stories – yes – and those that were our favourites – yes – but also ensuring we bought you a gloriously varied selection of stories. And variety is what you will find here: a mix of long and short short stories, a mix of themes taking in both supernatural horror and natural (all too human) horror, stories that are set in the past, the present and sometimes the near-future – all from an international mix of authors.

I won't go into any detail about any of the stories here as it's far better you read them for yourself. However, I am going to have to mention one because I was persuaded that I should include a story of my own here. I didn't do this with *The Second Corona Book of Horror Stories*, but my story "Ticks" – about which some people said some nice things – was included in the original *Corona Book of Horror Stories*. And in fairness, "Cancer the Crab", my story in this book, is a very, very short story – a mere 500 words – so it's not taking the place of a full story from anyone else.

In this book, as with other Corona Books anthologies, we've chosen to keep the stories in their respective authors' native version, or their choice of national version, of English. So, you will find stories by American authors presented in American English and so on. Elsewhere this book is presented in British English (where we have colours, sceptics and centres rather than colors, skeptics and centers etc.) Although it's sometimes quite subtle, the international differences extend to punctuation too, and so, for example, we've respected the fact that Americans favour the use of double quotes for speech, whereas we Brits, it seems, prefer single quotes when it comes to fiction in print.

In case of interest and as an aid to readers who might want to check out other writing from the authors of their favourite stories in this book, at the end of the book you'll also find short biographies for all the contributors, along with a listing of Twitter accounts and author websites for those that have them.

We truly hope you enjoy reading *The Third Corona Book of Horror Stories*, and if so, all our efforts will have been worthwhile.

Now, on with the (horror) show!

Lewis Williams
Withernsea, Summer 2019

SUDS AND MONSTERS

Christopher Stanley

Gavin stares at the thick layer of foam bobbing on top of the water in the sink. The way it moves, the gentle rise and fall, it could almost be breathing.

'Just do the damn dishes,' his stepmum said before she left. 'And don't make me ask you again.' Even when she's out, her voice seems to follow him around the house, droning on about the many ways in which he lets his family down. Hardly a day passes without her complaining about his attitude or the amount of dirty laundry he's failed to put in the wash basket. And she hates it when he doesn't do the washing up.

Behind him, on the island in the middle of the kitchen, there's a tower of dirty crockery. Crusted plates from last night's bangers and mash. Sticky bowls from lunchtime's pasta. It is Gavin's turn to wash up, but it's just so boring. His parents used to be happy as long as he was playing quietly. Then his mum moved out and everything went to hell.

He's about to put a dish in the water when something breaks the surface, like a fish in a pond. He leans closer, watching a million tiny bubbles wobble and pop. There could be anything in the sink and he wouldn't know. He takes a carving knife from the block and carefully slices through the foam, but it doesn't help. He swishes it from side to side, creating temporary lagoons, thinking maybe he was mistaken, when in one of the foamless gaps he spots something sliding across the bottom.

Something alive.

Holding the knife with both hands, he counts down from five and stabs it into the water. Nothing. With his heart thumping in his chest, he raises it again, counts down and stabs. The tip of the blade finds the hard metal base of the sink but nothing else. He lifts the knife one more time, studying the movement of the water, poised like a fisherman with a spear, lord of the suds, grand master of the washing up. And then he strikes, the blade slicing through the foam, water splashing up as far as his elbow, and something else, something slimy and unexpected, which curls around his right arm and snaps tight.

Gavin lets out a wail of surprise and his voice comes back to him, echoing around the empty house. The thing, whatever it is, tugs him forward, trying to pull him into the sink. He fights it, thrashing and splashing soap suds everywhere, his shirt sleeves wet to the shoulder, his wrist singing with pain. He grabs for the carving knife, thinking he might be able to cut himself free, but the thing tugs him back into the sink and the carving knife flies from his hand. His arm is pinned tight, his flesh stretched and squeezed until he's in too much pain to cry out. Blindly, he gropes with his free hand, clutching at the worktop, the washing machine, searching for anything with a decent edge, desperately trying to find enough leverage to pull his arm free. But the thing is too damn powerful.

Upstairs, immediately above his head, the water pipes

groan. His dad always blamed this on air in the system, but it doesn't sound like air. It sounds like anger.

As the water drains from the sink, Gavin can see the thing more clearly, enough to know it's some sort of tentacle, translucent and eel-like, that's punched its way through the plughole. It stinks of rotting fish and ammonia, a noxious cocktail that makes his stomach turn. He claws at it, digging his nails in, and it seems to be yielding when lights flash in his eyes and pain shoots up his left arm. The tentacle has bitten a deep triangle of flesh from the tip of his thumb. A single drop of his blood drips into what's left of the washing-up water and hangs, suspended, blooming like a jellyfish. He stares in horror as a black, wiry hair sprouts from the side of the tentacle, looping towards his blood and sucking it up. More hairs start to grow, dozens of them, feeling for the pores in his arm and burrowing into his flesh. Each one hurts like a bee sting, and he cries out in agony. Blinking the tears from his eyes, he watches in horror as the hairs slide around under his flesh, searching for blood.

The tentacle turns red and the room melts away. In its place is a mountain of throbbing, slimy flesh. Eyes like hot air balloons, bulging with anger and madness. Purple-grey tentacles the size of freight trains. The air is filled with the stench of decay and the sound of wet flesh squelching over wet flesh. And the worst thing is Gavin can feel it, the monster, from the deathly thump of its heart to the tip of every tentacle. He can run his fingers over the scars of its memories: bred to suffer; trapped between dimensions; starved and tortured in some distant, hellish realm until its hunger and pain manifest themselves in the water tanks and sewers of Earth.

Anywhere there's a soft spot. The more the creature is exposed to violence, the more it slips through.

Soon it will be everywhere.

A fresh wave of pain drags Gavin back into the kitchen, and he cries out for help. He tells himself this can't be happening. It can't be real. Every time he tries to pull himself free, the tentacle tightens its grip. He searches for a weapon but can't reach any further than the plant pots and plastic jugs on the windowsill, or the tea bags and cereal in the wall cupboard. Then he remembers the carving knife, which he dropped to the floor earlier. He leans towards it, left arm outstretched, but he's nowhere near. When he tries to hook it with his foot, the millimetres between his toes and the blade might as well be miles.

The kitchen starts to melt away again and he can feel himself slipping back into the creature's mind. He's halfway gone when the backdoor opens and his stepsister enters the house, lipstick pretty, coat buttoned up to her chin and carrier bags banging against her jeans. 'If it's positive,' she says to her phone, 'I'm going to kill myself. Mum'll freak if she finds out. You think I want his spawn growing inside me?' When she sees Gavin, she cups her hand over the phone and whispers, 'Tell anyone and I'll kill you.'

'Becky,' he says.

She holds her palm up to him, not even slowing down.

'Help me!' he shouts after her. 'Becky, please!'

She's already heading up the stairs, rattling a small cardboard box and saying, 'As if my life isn't miserable enough already. This is all I need.'

Gavin calls for her again, but his voice is too weak. He

tugs feebly at the tentacle, but it won't budge. Through the ceiling, he hears his stepsister peeing into the toilet bowl – the noise going on and on – until she stops abruptly, gasps and starts to scream. Gavin hears water gushing, toothbrushes clattering and other noises that make no sense at all. Then everything goes quiet. He waits, hardly daring to breathe, hoping his stepsister will call out to reassure him that she's okay, but all he hears is a deathly thump, which shakes the ceiling and causes dust to rain down from the kitchen lights. He shouts her name, over and over, until the water pipes growl threateningly in response. It's a deep, guttural moan that silences everything.

Exhausted, he slumps against the kitchen worktop.

* * *

'You little bastard.'

Gavin opens his eyes and squints through layers of headache to see his stepmum in the kitchen, a creased and faded version of her daughter, stubbing her cigarette out in a mug.

'After everything I've done for you,' she says. 'I asked you to do one thing, just one thing, and this is how you thank me. Look at this mess.'

The floor's all wet and the tower of crockery is as tall as it ever was. In the sink, the tentacle is still wrapped around his arm but it's translucent again. Something else has slaked its thirst.

'I'm going to do you a favour and tell you the truth,' says his stepmum, oblivious to the tentacle. 'I don't want you here anymore. None of us do. You just don't belong in this house.'

'Help me,' he whispers.

'Look at this,' she says, picking up the carving knife and sliding it across the worktop. 'What *have* you been up to?'

He stares at her, remembering all the times she's made him feel unwanted, all the names she's called his real mum and all the nasty little ways she's made his dad miserable. Like when she gave his CD collection to the charity shop because 'they're all on the computer now.' And when she dropped his phone into his drink because he refused to delete his ex-wife's number. *Enough*, thinks Gavin. He could warn her. He could tell her there's a monster in the pipes. Instead, he says, 'Becky's taking a pregnancy test in the bathroom.'

His stepmum freezes. Her eyes say no, it can't be true, not my daughter, not my precious, innocent, *virgin* daughter. Then she hurries through the lounge and disappears up the stairs.

In the kitchen, Gavin takes a deep, steadying breath and reaches for the carving knife. As he prepares to cut himself free, he listens to his stepmum entering the bathroom and wonders if she'll scream the same way her daughter did.

THE DEBT

John Haas

Gary's eyes drifted open again. This time it appeared consciousness would stay, at least for a short while. His blurry vision grasped onto things only to lose them a moment later. His arm. An overhead light. Part of the bed. He twisted his head to the left and was rewarded with everything going dull grey.

With maddening slowness his world came back, resolving into the circle of light that surrounded him, followed by a deeper blackness beyond.

He attempted to pull his arms up to his face only to find they wouldn't move. Were they tied down? He looked toward his feet, but his somewhat ample belly got in the way as an indistinct, lumpy blur.

"Hello?" he shouted, words leaving his dry mouth as a whisper. He hadn't known how thirsty he was until he tried to speak. "Hello?" he tried again, still with no volume.

The first tendrils of panic seeped into him. He was groggy, couldn't think straight. Was he in a hospital? He could smell that clean, antiseptic odor he associated with hospitals. If he was, then why...? Why what? No, he'd lost the thread of thought. Forget it, he'd come back to it.

Something else. A party. Yes, there *had* been a party,

for him, and he'd gotten drunk. First week out and he'd gotten drunk. Had there been an accident? Was that why he was here?

Why had he done it? He already knew the answer to that one. He was weak for booze and it was that simple. If there'd been an accident, it would be no secret that he had been drinking. Even if he hadn't been behind the wheel, he was sunk.

Despair covered him like grave dirt.

So stupid. Gary had sworn those days were in the past, but all he needed to break his vow were the guys at his door with armloads of booze. He had every reason in the world to not start drinking again, but he'd done it anyway. He'd made a mess of his life. Again. So soon.

Leaving prison, he had thought about getting out of town and starting a new life where no one knew him, but the conditions of his parole wouldn't let him. He should have just—

"Mr. Jones," a man's voice interrupted, making Gary flinch, "happy to see you back with us." The owner of the voice stepped into the light. The man was tall and slim and wore a white doctor's coat with one nice, expensive gold pen in the left breast pocket.

He knew this man from somewhere. "Where am I?" Gary croaked.

"What was that, Mr. Jones? I'm afraid I didn't quite hear you."

Gary cleared his throat. His mouth was so dry.

"Where—" he tried again.

The doctor was already nodding. "Yes, I imagine you would have a question or two."

The man put a straw into Gary's mouth and allowed

him a sip of water before pulling it away. Gary wanted to object but still didn't have a voice.

"Not too much," the doctor said. "Not yet."

He examined Gary with simple clinical detachment. "You have questions for me, but there will be time for that later. For now, let the anaesthetic wear off."

Gary started to protest, but even with his fear and confusion, he felt himself sliding away again.

"Not to worry, Mr. Jones. Nothing will happen without you." It could have been the comforting line a doctor told a patient, but it was said without a trace of emotion.

Gary watched the doctor fade away. That face. He *knew* that face. It was... What? Older? Yes, but that wasn't all. Tired too. But those eyes hadn't changed.

"Who are you?" Gary managed, his eyes drooping.

"Sleep," the voice said. "We'll talk later."

Gary was gone again.

* * *

He faded in and out, or at least he thought he did. Somewhere in that time his mind made a connection and he started to dream.

He was back in the courtroom. The rows of seats behind the benches were full, all the way back to the wide double doors. Strangers mostly. All here less for what he had done than because of who his father was. Ironic. After the accident his father wanted nothing to do with him, didn't even show up for the trial. No, his father had to distance himself from his embarrassing liability of a son if he ever hoped of running for mayor.

Not much of a trial anyway. The public defender had explained the evidence against him and suggested if he pled guilty he might get a lighter sentence, especially if Gary showed he was willing to seek help for his drinking. Gary had argued. What if he told his story as sympathetically as possible? It wasn't his fault. The road conditions. His brakes. The other driver.

No. His lawyer explained how that trial would go. Gary would give his sympathetic testimony; then the officer who first arrived on the scene would tell how Gary's blood alcohol level was .25 – more than three times the legal limit. The paramedics would be next telling how Gary's monster SUV had caved in the side of the other vehicle so it was close to U-shaped; how Gary had gotten through without a scratch while they needed to amputate the boy's right arm just to get him out of the car; how the boy died calling for his mother before they could get him to the ambulance. If any of the family got on the stand, like the uncle who had been driving, well…

Gary had insisted on a trial anyway.

Nobody likes a lawyer unless they're being defended by one, and most times not even then. The fact that his father was a lawyer hurt him; that his father was a high-priced lawyer that defended corporate scumbags and squashed the little man hurt more. Gary being in law school was viewed as following in his old man's footsteps down the road of scumbaggery. None of it bought him an ounce of sympathy.

His lawyer had been right; the prosecution creamed him. At the end of the first day Gary stood before the judge and changed his plea to guilty.

And throughout it all a tall, thin, well-dressed man sat

in the first row just behind the prosecutor, staring at Gary. He never showed any emotion and his eyes never wavered. When Gary had his back to the crowd he could feel those eyes boring into him.

* * *

Gary's eyes shot open. The doctor stood next to him.

"I remember you," Gary whispered.

The man nodded. "You killed my son."

Gary shook his head and pulled on his restraints in a surge of panic. He could see them now. Thick brown leather straps at least three inches wide held each of his wrists, another one across his chest and more across his legs by the feel of it.

"I gave you something to force the anaesthetic from your system." The man glanced at the IV bottle to Gary's left, its tube winding down to the back of his hand. "You won't be slipping off again."

"It was an accident," Gary blurted, his stock excuse. "A stupid accident."

The doctor contemplated Gary for a moment, eyes boring into him. Gary had the distinct impression the man was peering through him and deep into his soul.

"Stupid? Oh yes, it was very stupid. But an accident? No, Mr. Jones, an accident is when your car slides on the ice. An accident is when your brakes fail. An accident is something out of your control. When you get drunk then drive your car that's no accident."

Gary's eyes slid away from the doctor. He still couldn't see anything outside of the circle of light.

"Vehicular manslaughter, they called it," the man continued.

Gary shrugged, agreeing with the man. Why not? The verdict was a matter of public record; he couldn't deny it now. He *had* been drunk and a boy had died in a car crash. All other details were irrelevant.

"Joshua was ten years old, an entire life ahead of him."

The sadness in the man's voice made Gary turn back. Tears brimmed the edge of the man's eyes for a moment; then they were gone.

"I'm sorry," Gary said.

"Are you?" The man leaned closer, any trace of emotion now gone. "Or are you sorry you got caught? Sorry that you had to go to jail for a short while?"

"Hey, I spent two *years* in prison," Gary spat out, now angry, "two *long* years of my life."

"Two *long* years? And yet, you still have a lifetime ahead of you, while my son is still dead. You didn't even serve the full five-year sentence."

"You don't know what I went through in there, what they did to me." Gary latched on to the phrase the judge had used when sentencing him. "I paid my debt to society."

The man stared at him for a moment. "Yes, you've paid your debt to society, Mr. Jones – such as it is – but you still owe."

Gary shook his head.

"Oh yes. You owe a debt to my son and to myself. You—"

"I'm sorry," Gary blurted, thinking it sounded more genuine this time.

"No, Mr. Jones, you don't know sorry. Not yet."

How could he convince this man that he was indeed

sorry? Tears welled in his eyes, tears of fear but surely this man would take them as regret.

The man leaned close to Gary's ear and whispered, "No, Mr. Jones, if you were truly sorry, you wouldn't have gotten drunk with your friends last night."

Gary couldn't meet the man's eyes. He'd had every intention of following the terms of his parole. He wasn't allowed to enter a bar or have a drink, not even at home, but all it took to forget were the guys at his door with some alcohol. He'd tried to keep the drinking moderate, but it had been two years since he'd had a drink. Yeah, he was weak for booze, but who kept putting it in front of him?

It wasn't his fault. None of it. Now he was here. The reality of his situation sunk in. He was trapped and *no one* knew where he was. Gary pulled with frantic strength on the restraints, feeling no give.

"What's this debt?" Gary asked, hearing and hating the panicky whine in his voice. "I don't have any money." Gary would never see another dime of the family money; that message was clear. Still, maybe his dad would pay off the ransom when he got the demand. He couldn't very well abandon his son in a way that would hurt the old political career.

"No money?" the man's soft voice asked. "Nothing? Not even a secret account?"

Gary's mouth opened, then snapped shut.

"Have no fear, Mr. Jones. I'm not interested in money." His lips twitched, and for a moment Gary thought the man might smile. It made his insides shrivel.

"I don't imagine you're much of a reader of Shakespeare, are you?"

"I – what?"

"Shakespeare, Mr. Jones. The bard."

Gary shook his head. He knew who Shakespeare was but hadn't read any since high school.

The doctor shook his head too. "No, I'm not surprised. No matter. Only one play concerns us: *The Merchant of Venice*. Do you know it?"

"Heard of it."

"Good. Well, most of that story is irrelevant to our situation, but the part with Shylock is quite germane." The man paused, obviously expecting Gary's input. When Gary shrugged he sighed and continued. "Shylock was a money lender, what today we would call a loan shark. Antonio and Bassanio, the heroes of the story, go to him because Bassanio needs to borrow money. Now, Shylock doesn't much like Antonio because of some comments he's made against money lenders."

The man walked to the edge of the light and reached for something in the darkness. While he talked, he wheeled a cart back to the side of Gary's table and stopped where Gary could see it. A thin square of fabric covered odd bumps and lumps on the cart.

"Shylock offers to loan the money to Bassanio and he even does it interest free. There is a catch, though. You see, if Bassanio defaults on the loan, then Shylock gets a special payment from Antonio."

The man folded back the fabric exposing a full table of gleaming surgical scalpels, saws, and utensils that Gary couldn't begin to identify. Terror splashed into Gary's brain.

"Shylock's payment would be a pound of Antonio's flesh."

The man stopped, observing Gary with that same lack of emotion.

"You're not serious," Gary whispered, feeling his voice desert him again. His eyes darted from the doctor to the surgical instruments and back. In a frenzy, he pulled on the restraints but only succeeded in emphasising his helplessness.

"Now in the play," the man continued, "Shylock would have chosen the pound of flesh, but in this case I will allow you to decide. It is, after all, your currency."

The man covered the instruments with the fabric again.

"As an example, a hand is about a pound, so is a foot."

"You're out of your mind," Gary said.

The doctor was quiet a long moment, focusing on something beyond Gary. "Perhaps. The loss of a child can do monumental damage to a parent's mind." He turned and headed for the surrounding blackness. "My sanity does not change your situation."

"Wait a god-damn minute," Gary yelled at the retreating man. "What if I refuse to play your game?"

"Then I will make your choice for you," the man replied over his shoulder. "You have fifteen minutes, Mr. Jones."

* * *

Insane.

The man was out of his friggin' mind. His kid's death had sent him over the edge and Gary was stuck in a nightmare, one he couldn't wake up from. No! No, there was always a way out of things – he just had to think of it. Think! Okay, so he didn't read Shakespeare for fun, but that didn't mean he was an idiot. He'd had an education. He had knowledge. He always beat them at the bar when *Jeopardy* came on.

The bar.

Shit, he sure could use a drink. He *needed* one the way a drowning man needs air. It would settle his nerves, help him think. But that was the whole problem, wasn't it? Not just the drinks from that night when the kid died but the ones from last night that he hadn't refused. He couldn't resist; he was too weak. He joined that group in prison, some kind of AA thing, but he'd just gone through the motions to show how repentant he was. It was easy to fake with no alcohol around.

Tears spilled down the side of his face. It wasn't his fault. None of it. That night. The booze. His car. Not his fault.

He shook off the pity. There was no time. The doctor would be back in a few minutes. What could he do, though?

"Play the game."

His own voice surprised him as much as finding that an idea had started to form. Gary would play the game, but by his own rules.

* * *

The doctor returned showing no sign of satisfaction, but Gary imagined he could feel it. The man had been watching him from the shadows; he was sure of it. Well, screw him and his dead kid.

"Have you made a choice, Mr. Jones?"

Gary cleared his throat. "I guess I have." He forced his

eyes to meet the doctor's. "Before I give you my choice, I want to know I'll be alive after you remove my—" Gary took a deep breath and went on. "After you remove the pound of flesh."

The man's mask cracked for a moment, a brief display of surprise.

"Well, yes of course."

"You promise?"

"I find it interesting that you are willing to accept the promise of a man who has confined you to a hospital bed, a man who *you* said was out of his mind. You put your trust in strange places."

Gary's resolve wavered.

"Nevertheless, for what it's worth," the man replied, "I promise you will be alive after the operation is over. You see, whatever your choice might be, I want you to live with it for the rest of your life. Each time you look in the mirror you will think of my son."

"And you'll let me go."

"After your debt has been paid you will be released, yes."

Gary eyed the room – the darkness, the overhead lights, and the tray of covered surgical tools in particular. His arms were starting to get numb and his back hurt from lying in the same position. He let out a long sigh and kept staring at the tray. "You're a surgeon?"

"I was."

"Was?"

"Yes." His voice was far away. "After Joshua I couldn't operate anymore. Everyone looked like him, each patient I couldn't save a vicious reminder and each one I could a slap in the face."

Gary wondered about his chances.

"Don't worry, Mr. Jones, I still remember how to cut something out of a person's body."

"I'm sure you do. One more question." Gary paused for dramatic effect. He'd steered the doctor to this point and now he had him. He savoured the smug satisfaction of knowing he'd won. "How much does an appendix weigh?"

Gary already knew the answer, a bit of knowledge from some trivia game. He'd gotten the promise from the man knowing that the doctor would be bound by whatever bizarre honour he was following. A ghost of a grin started to cross Gary's face. He'd won!

The man considered Gary a moment, his eyes wandering up and down. "In a person of normal weight an appendix would weigh about a third of a pound."

Gary's stomach dropped and the smugness vanished.

"But," the doctor continued, "in the morbidly obese it could weigh as much as six. In your case, Mr. Jones, I would guess your appendix could weigh around a pound, maybe a bit more."

"Okay, fine, that's my choice then. You can have my appendix. There's my pound of flesh."

The doctor was quiet, with a strange expression that Gary imagined to be surprise or respect. Gary had found a way out and all he'd given up was a useless organ.

"My appendix," he repeated, not attempting to disguise his smile.

* * *

Gary tried to find ways to distract himself while time crept by. With each minute, he became more apprehensive about the coming operation. To Gary's surprise a nurse came in, preparing the room for the operation, arranging surgical instruments. Didn't she realize Gary was a prisoner? Did she not understand the insanity going on here?

"Hey," he whispered, "help me. Please."

The nurse injected something into the IV line that ran into the back of his hand. She stepped forward and gave the needle in his hand a quick twist.

He hissed with the sudden pain. "What was that for?"

She turned away, but did he see a brief sneer on her face? Maybe. Fuck it. It would all be over soon.

Gary forced himself to lie still and close his eyes. After the operation, he would be on his way, the doctor had promised him. One thing Gary knew was liars. The doctor said he would let Gary go once his debt was paid and that was what would happen.

His debt! Jesus, now he was thinking that way.

When he got out of here, he would take some of that money in his Cayman Islands account and get the hell out of the country – should have done it already. He didn't care about his parole agreement. He would go somewhere they would never find him.

Then the room started to swim.

* * *

"Scalpel."

A dream.

"Scalpel," a feminine voice replied.

He heard the scrape of metal utensil against metal tray, then felt the pressure of a sharp knife cutting into the flesh of his lower right abdomen. There wasn't pain, not exactly, but there was a sensation, a feeling.

No. Not a dream. Not a god-damn dream at all.

He tried to talk, tried to open his eyes, tried to tell the doctor that he was still awake and aware of what was going on. He couldn't move, couldn't make a sound.

"Suction."

"Suction," the nurse replied.

Gary heard the sucking sound of a vacuum in liquid. *His* liquid.

He was helpless. Panic struck him, taking hold of his senses and scrambling his thoughts. The heart monitor's beeps rose.

"How are his vitals?"

"Within the limits," the nurse replied again.

Gary couldn't do anything, couldn't think past what was happening to him. Step by step he experienced them going through the operation. He would feel the occasional pressure inside as the doctor moved through his body, isolating his healthy organ and removing it. Gary had never felt so vulnerable in his life.

This wasn't how… This was…

"Suture."

"Suture."

As the sutures tied Gary's flesh closed, the world slipped away and he slept.

* * *

"I was aware of the whole operation. Everything. Every cut. Every sound. Every word said. Everything!" Tears rolled down his face and he knew he was hysterical.

"Anaesthesia awareness occurs in less than one percent of all patients. It's quite rare and an interesting subject in its own right."

Gary looked away from that emotionless face. He had no fascination in the medical side of what had happened. He wanted to run, to get far away from this man and his eyes, from this insanity and from his own memory.

"However, in this case I gave you a muscle relaxant to paralyze you and a pain killer so you wouldn't die."

Gary spun his head back.

"Oh yes, it was intentional, Mr. Jones. I *want* you to remember it. All of it."

The panic in his mind ramped up. He felt violated in a way he never suspected possible.

"Now, I know what you're waiting for," the doctor said.

The nurse wheeled a scale on a table up to Gary's bed and the doctor reached into a metal bin beside it. He pulled out a pinkish bloody mess that could only have been Gary's appendix and put it on the flat tray of the scale.

The urge to run spiked inside Gary's head while the digital display rolled upwards.

"A little over one pound, Mr. Jones."

"Keep the change," Gary muttered, trying to sound in control.

The doctor removed Gary's organ from the scale and put it back in the metal bin.

"It's done. My debt to your son has been paid." Gary wanted to add "you psychotic bastard" but held back – time for that later. With effort, he forced his eyes to lock with the other man's. "Now let me out of here."

The doctor shook his head back and forth while holding Gary's gaze.

"You promised," Gary yelled. "You lied."

"No, Mr. Jones. I meant it when I said you would be released after your debt had been paid."

Gary didn't understand him in the least.

"Your debt hasn't been paid yet."

Gary's eyes flicked to the now empty scale with a smear of his blood, then back again. The doctor nodded.

"Yes, that was your debt to my son. If you remember, I also said you had a debt to me."

The room spun and receded.

"You have fifteen minutes to make your decision."

* * *

Gary stared at nothing in particular, numb and unbelieving. He had to do it again. Minutes ago he had been confident, smug even, sure that he had beaten the doctor at his own game. Now he wasted several minutes in denial, panic threatening to engulf him. He needed to calm down.

He needed to tell the doctor the truth.

No! Absolutely not.

That helped him get a grip. He still couldn't focus on a choice, but the panic receded.

Breathe in. Breathe out. Focus on something else.

Gary tried to get into a more comfortable position but was stopped by the restraints again, and that tiny thing was one thing too much. He screamed into the room, partly for release and partly to hear his own voice. For the next few minutes Gary screamed and cried and begged. A sutured wound on his lower stomach said he had earned the right.

But if he didn't stop, that crazy bastard would come back and…

Gary spent more time forcing himself to calm down. He thought about good things like parties and girls and food and alcohol; pushing shadowed, grisly thoughts of operations out of his mind. Once he could focus without bringing the panic back he began to catalogue his body, starting at his head and working his way down considering each part in turn.

"I'm sure you have given it a good deal of thought, Mr. Jones," the doctor said emerging from the darkness.

Gary jumped as much as the restraints allowed.

"Before you tell me your choice, let me point out that your gall bladder, spleen, adenoids, tonsils and wisdom teeth together do not add up to a pound. Also, that second kidney of yours only weighs about a third of a pound."

"No. No, no, no. That wasn't fifteen minutes." He hated the pleading sound of his voice. Losing control by himself was one thing, but in front of this man…

The doctor gazed at Gary with his usual lack of emotion.

"I need more time. Please. Just a few minutes."

"If you don't have a choice—"

"No, I do. I do."

The doctor waited. Gary struggled to think of something, anything. His mind was frozen in a loop that kept returning to his foot, a choice he didn't want to make.

"Very well, Mr. Jones." The doctor headed for the darkness.

Gary had no doubt that the doctor was serious about making the decision for him. "No wait, please... I..."

The doctor had reached the light's edge when Gary's mind flipped over in one amazing moment of clarity, like flicking the switch in an unlit room. He had his answer.

And, Jesus Christ, it was so obvious.

"Can you do liposuction?" he blurted as the dimness swallowed the doctor.

Gary kept his eyes on the spot where the tall man had disappeared. For long, eternal moments nothing happened; then the man stepped back into view. He paused a moment before coming closer.

Liposuction *was* so obvious. It should have been his first choice. He berated himself for being so stupid and almost missing it a second time. The only excuse he had was that he never gave any thought to being overweight; it was just a part of him.

The doctor's eyes strolled to Gary's gut. A stomach that came from a love of food and beer. Even in prison he'd been able to get food when he wanted it, working on kitchen duty where the inmates got extras.

"Yes, Mr. Jones, I would be able to perform that procedure." The doctor's face didn't change. "You offer your fat as payment?"

"I do," Gary said, his smug confidence reclaimed. He'd foxed the man at his own game a second time.

* * *

As it was the last time, he was aware of all that went on around him. The sounds of the doctor and nurse preparing for the operation worried him. He had no idea what to expect, although he imagined liposuction must involve some sort of a vacuum pump. Even awake it shouldn't be *that* traumatic.

"Scalpel."

"Scalpel," the nurse replied.

He felt the pressure of a knife cutting through the skin on one side of his body and travelling in a horizontal arc to the opposite side.

What the hell?

The incision slanted upward and made its way back across his body, this time above the belly-button.

His skin was lifted.

"Suction," the doctor said.

"Suction."

No. No, no, no, no, no.

Over the next few hours Gary's skin and fat were pulled and lifted, a scalpel inserted underneath to detach the flesh from the abdominal wall.

He wanted to scream, to move, but he couldn't do anything except listen, and think. The worst moment was feeling the wide section of flesh pulled away from him and deposited into a container with a horrible, wet splat that would echo inside his head forever. Two edges of skin that had never met before were pulled together.

"Suture."

"Suture," the nurse repeated as Gary was finally allowed to slip away.

* * *

His dreams weaved in and out of the vague memories of the night that had changed his life, what details he remembered anyway. Him and Scotty getting in his car, laughing about something. A blur of headlights. His hands shooting up to grab the panic bar above the door. Scott lying on the ground and closing his eyes. Gary drifting around the accident listening to, but not quite hearing, the screams.

* * *

Awareness came back. Gary's eyes fluttered open to take in the now familiar ring of light and the doctor. He had a curious feeling of emptiness. Lifting his head to look down shot a vicious blast of pain through his mid-section. In that brief glimpse he saw he was thinner. A wide bandage spread from one hip to the other across his lower stomach, below where his belly-button should have been.

"That wasn't liposuction," Gary said.

"No, Mr. Jones, it was not."

"You said you would do lipo."

"No, I said I *could*. The operation *I* performed is called abdominoplasty. A tummy tuck in layman's terms."

"But, why—"

"Mr. Jones, I said you could choose the pound of flesh to pay with. I never said you could choose how I would collect it."

A chill crept through Gary's soul.

"I removed as much fat as possible from your body," the doctor said, reaching with his arm outside Gary's field of vision. "Now, let's see how much all of that fat weighed."

The cart rolled into Gary's line of sight and he clenched his eyes. "Please."

"Very well, Mr. Jones," the doctor said, "let's just say you gave more than enough."

Gary expected a trick, but when he opened his eyes there was only the doctor in front of him. "Okay. I've paid my debt to your son, and now I've paid my debt to you."

The doctor made no movement.

"Look, I'm sorry for what happened, okay!" Gary was surprised to find it was true. "You've taught me a lesson. I'm sorry. Just, please let me go."

The doctor's head gave an almost imperceptible shake.

"I promise I won't tell anyone about this. Please."

"In time, Mr. Jones."

"You promised."

"Yes, as soon as your debt is paid."

Gary's skin crawled and the hairs on his arms stood up in abject fear. He started to sob. "My debt…"

The doctor beckoned and the nurse came into the light to stand beside the man. She looked Gary in the face and he saw it. Where the doctor had an emotionless, piercing stare she had deep pools of soul-scorching hate. Her expression would have made him recoil if he could move.

"She—"

"Is my wife, Joshua's mother."

Gary looked at the nurse, at her hateful glare, the tears in her eyes.

"You probably don't recognize her. She couldn't bear to be at your trial."

Gary's eyes travelled from one to the other and back again.

"You will next pay your debt to her."

"My debt—"

"Is not yet paid, Mr. Jones."

"No." Gary shook his head. "No! You took more than a pound when you took my fat. You took extra."

"Yes, Mr. Jones. That was your debt to me and it's been paid, overpaid as you've stated. Your debt to my wife must be paid separately."

Gary shot a look of blistering hatred at the doctor and lay his head back, staring at the ceiling. After a moment he realized the two hadn't moved. Gary turned back to them.

"My wife wants to choose which body part to take."

No. That loathing in her eyes... she would take his head.

"It is her right, as a mother," the doctor explained.

"Please, no."

"No," the doctor agreed. "I convinced her there was more justice in you choosing. However, if you can't come up with a choice—"

"I'll take your arm." The woman completed. "The right one. From your shoulder."

* * *

Gary was out of options. He was out of hope, out of luck and very soon out of time.

"Relax. Breathe in and out slowly."

He closed his eyes and searched for a calm he wasn't sure was there. Bit by bit, he backed away from the edge of panic. He didn't think about doctors, operations, organs or debts. No, that wasn't true. He did think of one debt. Scotty owed him huge. He would be visiting good old Scotty Everhart and his dad after getting out of here. Right after he visited the cops.

"Enough. Come back to that later."

He kept his focus on the nothing occupying his mind, pushing the calm until he knew he had a firm grasp of it.

Now, think.

Starting at the feet he worked his way up. He could give part of his stomach or intestine, but that seemed more horrible than what *she* wanted. Gary went through all of the needless and extra body parts several times. Together they wouldn't add up to a pound, just as the doctor had said.

I removed as much fat as possible from your body.

Now Gary knew why. The doctor didn't want Gary using the fat to pay again. All that fat! He could have paid a hundred debts with what he had given. Gary could feel the flabby skin rubbing painfully, which was the point he was sure. His thighs. His chest. His ass. The doctor had done his job well. Gary was awake and aware. No weakness or nausea. No light-headedness. He was as fit as he had been last night, or close enough at least.

He wished he *could* pass out. Despair threatened to drag him down again and steal his fifteen minutes.

God damn it. Scotty should be on this table!

The doctor had come back into the circle of light at some point and stood next to the head of the bed. He couldn't have been there long.

"Mr. Jones." Not a question or a command, but a statement with an expectation of a response.

Gary thought about it. Did he tell this man the truth? No! He had spent two years in prison and kept his mouth shut with worse things happening to him. He wouldn't throw it all away now. Without that money… His eyes flicked away from the doctor, then back again. What other options did he have? He had run out of body parts to give away. He had to make a choice and right now or that crazy bitch would take his arm.

The doctor turned away.

"No, wait."

His voice was so low he was sure for a moment that it was only in his head, but the doctor stopped.

"Wait," Gary repeated.

The doctor's calm, unwavering eyes wore Gary down. "God damn it," he yelled, "you could at least show some joy at this revenge of yours. Wring your hands. Let out a mad cackle. Anything."

"Revenge, Mr. Jones? Revenge?" His lips twitched. "This isn't revenge. This is justice." "Now, your choice?"

Gary muttered something.

"I beg your pardon, Mr. Jones?"

"I said," Gary cleared his throat and met the doctor's eyes, "my foot. Take my left foot."

Gary twisted away, examining the other side of the bed. When he looked back the doctor was gone.

* * *

His mind floated in and out of the here and now, something which he was grateful for. He was aware of the doctor and his wife prepping him for the operation but kept his eyes closed and ignored them. He wouldn't give them any more satisfaction than he had to. The IV moved as they added something. Would they make him live through this operation too?

Screw it. It was worth it. He thought about the money and the secret he had carried the last three years.

Scotty had been driving Gary's SUV when they sailed through the red light at 100 mph and into the side of the other car.

The next day, Scotty's dad – the mayor – and their lawyer met with Gary at the jail. The lawyer slid a piece of paper with a long number written on it and a dollar sign at the front to Gary.

"That will be deposited to a Cayman Islands account in your name after the trial," the lawyer told him. "If you ever tell a soul what really happened, we will take back every cent."

Scotty's dad had bigger goals than being mayor. You could get into the White House if your son had been a passenger in an unfortunate accident but not if he had been the driver.

"Scott was asleep in the car the whole time and had no knowledge of what happened. Right, Gary?" the lawyer said.

Gary agreed to the deal before the lawyer had finished talking. That money would mean no more jumping to his father's cracked whip, no more pretending he wanted to be a lawyer. It didn't matter what the punishment was. They couldn't skin him alive.

Skin!

It came to him just like that. All of the flabby, painful skin the doctor had left behind, surely that would add up to a pound.

Gary tried to open his eyes.

* * *

As he swam out of the anaesthetic Gary became aware that he could still feel his left foot. He *had* told them about the skin in time. A strange happiness filled him and he felt like laughing. He'd beat them, stopped them at removing unnecessary parts and he would keep the money too. He moved his legs and was rewarded with a blinding blast of pain that tried to knock him out again. When his vision cleared Gary could see his right foot sloped up to where his toes poked against the inside of the sheet. On the left, no slope. Nothing.

Vague memories swirled. An operation. The sound of a saw— and that's where his mind cut off the memory, refusing to go further.

He tried to lift his leg, but the pain and nausea that slammed into him made him pass out instantly.

* * *

"Mr. Jones."

A voice from a long way off.

"Wake up, Mr. Jones."

Just a few more minutes.

A hard slap across his face and his eyes rolled behind the lids

Huh? What?

Another slap from the other side and his eyes opened. They refused to focus for a long moment but then locked in on the face of the nurse. She stood over him, a vague satisfaction in her eyes, hand drawn upwards. The doctor shook his head and the hand dropped.

"Good. You're awake," the doctor said.

He pulled the sheet back from Gary's left foot – from the place it used to be – and inspected Gary's stump. With a nod of satisfaction he dropped the sheet again. Behind Gary the nurse added something to his IV.

"Just an antibiotic, Mr. Jones," the man said.

"It's over," Gary muttered to the man. "It's paid."

Father, mother and son, all paid. Now all he wanted to do was sleep, to forget that he'd come up with the right decision too late. He didn't care about any of it. The kid. Scotty. The doctor. The money.

Nothing mattered.

The man looked at Gary with a stony silence that pulled him back from the abyss. Gary's eyes focused and sleep fled.

"It's done," he repeated.

The man raised his right hand and a light went on in the dark. An observation room with three young men, who stood watching.

Creeping horror swam through his body at the sight of the three. They stood so still they could have been mannequins.

"These are Joshua's brothers."

"No," Gary whisper-pleaded. "No, please no."

The doctor moved toward that one lighted room.

"No, listen. Please."

The doctor kept walking.

"I wasn't driving that night," Gary blurted in a rush. "I didn't kill your son. It was Scotty. Scott Everhart. He was the driver."

The man stopped, listening to the panicked ramblings until Gary was finished. "I know, Mr. Jones."

"What?"

The doctor turned back and examined Gary with quiet menace. "Mr. Everhart has paid his debt."

"But he… No!" Gary screamed. "Why? If you already knew, then why? Why are you doing this?"

"Why, Mr. Jones? Because of you, my son's killer went unpunished. Do I need a better reason?" With that, the doctor walked out of the light. "I'll be back for your three choices."

"No! I didn't do it! It wasn't me!"

Gary's head sank back against the bed and he looked around him. His mouth hung open as a brain-freezing, testicle-shrivelling realization came to him. There was enough room in the darkness for five more observation rooms.

OLD GODS

Sue Bentley

Cranby was sweating, the sourness of it prickling his groin and armpits. Dust penetrated the rag tied around his face and clogged his nose and throat. The tunnel sloped downwards, growing ever narrower.

Don't think of the weight of earth and stone above. Just keep going. He blinked gritty-eyed through the muddied lenses of his goggles, hoping he wouldn't encounter a blockage or come to a dead end. There was no room to turn around and he didn't have the energy to work all the way backwards. Elbows and knees worn ragged, he edged forward.

Sneaking out alone from the hut at base camp before Mayhew woke no longer seemed like such a good idea. Tropical rain had dripped through the palm-frond roof and in the humidity their beds had grown a fine covering of mould, but the suffocating heat of the hut was as nothing to the inside of the mountain. If he died here, buried beneath mud and powdered rock, his body might never be found. Panic bloomed in his gut. He began to choke and terror threatened to overwhelm him.

Cranby cared nothing for either religion or any creed except his own. But he cried out now, spit and mud bubbling on his lips in the sweating darkness. 'Dear Lord, deliver me. I'm a…a… bad man. A sinner, I know it. But I'm begging you. I'm not ready to die. Let me live and I'll pay back everyone I've cheated. Find those… I've deserted or harmed. Tell them I'm sorry…'

He stopped abruptly as his outstretched hand closed on emptiness. He had broken through. With renewed energy, he wormed forward until his head was uncovered. Dragging air into his lungs, he heaved his shoulders and then the rest of his body through the narrow opening and flopped onto a surface of smooth stone. Spent, he lay there gasping as relief washed over him. A draught came from somewhere. The air was clean and had a faintly metallic tang. He drew in great breaths of it, then hawked and spat to clear his nose and throat. He was really here, in the tomb. The first man to set foot inside since… well, forever. He savoured the moment of triumph, chest swelling with pride, before rising slowly to his feet.

Mayhew would be awake now. Having realised where Cranby must have gone, he'd have roused the bearers and set them to widening the head of the tunnel that plunged into the mountain. He wouldn't be far behind. An hour or two, possibly. A careful man was Mayhew, even ponderous. Cranby knew himself to be the risk-taker, not averse to spilling blood if the situation demanded it. He'd had failures aplenty. But not this time. His prayers had been answered.

He looked around. Faint light poured in from some-how high above. A dim graininess allowed him to see no more than a few feet in any direction before deep shadows swallowed his vision. Fumbling at his belt, he lit the torch and in the flare of it caught his breath. All around were carved pillars, joining with a vaulted ceiling that soared high overhead. It was like a cathedral; though plainly the builders of this place knew nothing of any God worshipped in his own world.

There were steps leading to a platform topped by a seated figure. Cranby's jaw dropped at the gleam of gold and precious stones. On a massive carved throne he sat, this priest-king or emperor. Who knew what he had been? His naked bones were stained dark red, like polished wood. From his shoulders hung a cloak of overlapping gold leaves. A gold mask inscribed with strange designs covered his head and shoulders, and was moulded closely to the dead man's features. Cranby leaned close to examine cheekbones, a jutting nose and a wide mouth. Two circles set with blue stones gave the impression of large staring eyes.

Lifting the torch, he turned full circle. Flickering light snagged on white domes. Skulls, everywhere. Rows and rows of them in niches set into the walls and on shelves, thousands of them, all with precious stones in eye sockets. The jewels glittered green, red and yellow, but only the king's mask bore the vibrant blue stone, said to be so prized by those who had once lived in the crumbling city deep in the forest at the base of the mountain.

Tears of the Gods, the bearers called it. Glowing rather than glittering, the blue stone was prized for its unique ability to bring eternal life. Hadn't done a lot for this dead king, had it? Cranby sniggered. Look at him, a bundle of bones beneath his cloak and mask. All that stuff about eternal life, ignorant superstition. But enough people believed it to make the stone valuable, and that was all that mattered. He already had buyers lined up for the Tears of the Gods.

Another laugh rasped in his throat. All the lean years of planning, begging and borrowing, of being in debt up to his neck, were over. From now on he'd live like a king, once he'd fobbed off that fool Mayhew with a tenth of what he was due. The thought of walking into his club and meeting with his financers and naysayers was sweet indeed. No one would ever again call Edward Cranby a hopeless dreamer or waste of breath.

He leaned forward, gave a mocking bow to the long-dead husk in the fabulous cloak and mask. 'You, my bony friend, are my salvation.'

A few days later, Cranby's initial elation had largely worn off. He woke from a restless sleep, his gaze alighting on the stacked boxes of precious stones and chunks of gold. They still had to transport the stuff to the coast. He wouldn't relax until it was safely aboard the ship, along with himself and Mayhew. It was raining again, drenching rods that soaked everything. The unremitting sound of it coupled with the constant screaming of birds and monkeys was enough to drive men to madness. It was never cooler after rain. If anything, the heat was worse – the forest steaming and clouds of insects swirling upwards. He was desperate to leave. After months of trekking through jungle, his boots had rotted on his feet and the skin peeled away. His body was covered with wounds from razor sharp grass and poisonous plants, and insect bites that had turned to ulcers and buried down to bone. He and Mayhew's bodies were wasted from fevers and lack of food, their supplies having run out months ago.

Heaving himself out of the bed, Cranby yawned and stretched. The fire had gone out and the tin pot in which they boiled drinking water was empty. He felt a stir of annoyance at having to stumble down to the river. Where the hell were the bearers? Was he also expected to find firewood and attempt to light a fire himself?

There were about a dozen bearers left, from the thirty who'd started out. A number had deserted after refusing to dig into the sacred mountain. Others had been lost to accident and disease. Cranby had bribed those who remained with extra money to risk their Gods' displeasure. Troublesome and superstitious, they might be, but they were hard workers, couldn't deny that. They'd seemed agitated lately, plainly as restless as he was to leave.

At some time between waking and sleeping, he'd heard a sound, like a roar and a gurgling scream. It must have been the cry of a great jungle cat, for the bearers had raised voices and beat staves on trees in an attempt to frighten the beast away. It was not far to the riverbank. He knelt in the mud to collect water, expecting Mayhew to appear at any moment. The man was probably squatting in the bush. Loose bowels were another thing that plagued them. Pushing himself to his feet, Cranby padded back to the makeshift camp, wincing as stones dug into his feet through their wrapping of rags.

In a moment of rare silence, he heard a pattering sound. Drops of some dark colour spotted the leaves and ground ahead of him. Yet another downpour beginning, he thought, walking faster towards the dubious shelter of the hut. A shadow slanted across his vision. He looked up, frowning. At first, he did not register what he was seeing. As realisation crashed in upon him, he gave a strangled cry and dropped the pot of water. It landed on one of his sore feet. Pain lanced through him, but he hardly felt it, all his attention focused on what was hanging from the tree.

Mayhew's feet were secured to a branch. His limp arms swayed in the air three feet or so above Cranby's head. Blood covered his face and chest, dripping down his bound arms and off the ends of his fingers. As the body slowly turned, he saw what had been done to it. Mayhew's eyes had been gouged out. In each of the sockets a jumble of red and green stones had been jammed. The man's mouth was wide open, gagged by larger stones. Two-inch-long thorns jabbed through Mayhew's bloodied flesh holding all in place.

Cranby gaped, open-mouthed, trembling and appalled. He recalled the cries he'd assumed were from a jungle cat, recognising them now as the sounds of Mayhew being tortured. He hadn't much cared for the man, but no one deserved to die like that. He was about to stumble away when a thin howl emerged from the suspended body.

Dear God. Mayhew was still alive.

Cranby felt the skin of his skull crawl. Bile rose in his throat and he dry-retched. Mayhew twitched and jerked while the terrible, muffled keening went on and on. A liquid, bubbling sound; the man was drowning in his own blood.

For endless moments, Cranby stood rooted, torn between horror and pity. Mayhew was beyond help; he could do nothing for him. Panic overcame him at the thought that the killers might still be close. Where were the remaining bearers? Had they been killed too? Should he look for them, at the risk of being caught and suffering a similar fate? He was defenceless and unarmed. What chance did he have?

In mortal fear of his life he set off at a shambling run, his one thought to get as far away as possible. He would leave everything, except for the small box with the Tears of the Gods inside. Crashing back to camp through bushes and trees, he stumbled against tree trunks, skinning his elbows and palms and losing all sense of direction. Finally, hopelessly lost, he tripped on a vine and measured his length on the jungle floor. His head struck something hard. Everything turned black…

Sometime later, Cranby's eyes fluttered open. With consciousness came pain and confusion. The darkness was slashed by torch-flame. Night again. He must have lain unconscious for hours. Dizziness filled him. There was burning pressure in his hands and feet, swaying movement. He was tied to a pole slung across the shoulders of a group of swiftly moving men. If they were the same ones who had killed Mayhew – for by now the man must surely be dead – why was he still alive? Hope followed Cranby's reasoning. There was a chance he could bargain with them. Money was one thing everyone understood.

'I have money. Lots of it. If you let me go, I'll pay you,' he said, his voice rough. 'I can make you rich.'

One of them answered. Cranby knew a little of the bearers' language, although Mayhew had done most of the communicating.

'We need no money.' The tall man was slightly better nourished-looking than his fellows. His name translated as Grass, Cranby recalled. It appeared Grass was the appointed leader.

'Why are you doing this?' Cranby said desperately. 'Have I not treated you well? I demand that you release me! Come on, fellow. You're a good man. You can stop this, Grass. Tell them, they'll be severely punished once this comes to light. You won't get away with it, none of you. Let me go now. And that'll be an end to it. I won't bring charges against you, I swear it. What do you say?'

Grass did not reply. Despite all entreaties, threats and finally insults, Cranby was borne swiftly along. Walls of crumbling stone flashed past his eyes as they wove through the city to the base of the mountain.

'Why are you bringing me here? I demand to know!'

'Be silent,' Grass said tonelessly.

Cranby could do nothing but endure. Every jolt sent agony coursing through his wrists and ankles. His back was on fire, and his neck hurt from trying to hold up his head so that it did not dash against the floor. At the concealed entrance to the tomb the bearers paused to remove barriers, before plunging into the mountain. Flares illuminated the way into the dead king's chamber.

Once there, Cranby's wrists and ankles were untied. Whimpering with pain as blood flowed back into cramped muscles, he was jerked to his feet and made to stand looking up at the gold throne.

Which was empty.

Cranby frowned in astonishment. Where were the skeletal remains of the king? He had removed the cloak and golden mask himself, while Mayhew stripped jewels from the eye sockets of row upon row of skulls. But he hadn't removed the king's bones, as far as Cranby knew neither had anyone else.

Grass reached for the sack slung across his shoulders. Opening it, he produced the gold mask which had covered the king's face. To Cranby's surprise he saw that the blue stones had been replaced. Another of the bearers came forward with an object, which he placed in an empty niche.

Cranby choked back a cry. It was Mayhew's head, bloodied and battered in contrast to the bleached white skulls.

At a dry rustling sound, the bearers turned in a single motion towards the entrance to a large alcove. All of them fell to their knees. Cranby's eyes bulged and the breath left his body. Emerging from the alcove was a tall, bronze-coloured skeleton. It slowly came forward, the bony feet scraping on stone.

Sweating with horror, Cranby stood rooted as the long-dead king moved to stand in front of him. Fleshless eye sockets bored into him, and he had the awful sensation that the thing could somehow see into his soul. Before he knew what was happening, two of the bearers gripped his arms. With no warning, the skeletal king reached out and plunged his index finger into Cranby's right eye.

Cranby howled. Fire and lightning ran up his spine as the king scooped his bony finger around his eye socket. His screams echoed in the burial chamber as liquid ran down his cheek. The soft weight of something fell onto his chest and continued downwards. His skull was held tightly from behind, so he could do nothing as a hard object was pressed into his raw and bleeding eye socket.

A blessed numbness followed, and impossibly he could see again from the ruined eye.

Sobbing, hardly able to catch his breath, he saw that something was happening to the skeletal king. Flowing downwards from the head, blood, muscle, sinew and organs were clothing the skull and bones. In a short time, the right side of the king's body was covered with skin that glowed with health. One side of the skeleton was now a slender well-made form, with half a handsome face and curling hair. In the centre was a sharp divide, a clean cut revealing red rawness and the outline of pulsing organs and vessels. In the ribcage, half a heart was beating strongly. On the handsome half-face the half-lips smiled, teeth gleaming. The single, bright blue eye gleamed.

Cranby's appalled gaze took in the impossibility of what was happening. Knowing what to expect, he cried out. 'No! No, please, don't! I'm begging you…'

His voice trailed off into a scream, which cracked on a high note as the half-king reached out a skeletal finger and jabbed it deep into his left eye. Half-fainting, Cranby sagged in the bearers' grip as once again one of his eye sockets was raked and all matter expelled. Once again, a hard object was placed in the raw socket and the pain ceased instantly. And once again his sight was restored.

Even though he knew what would happen, Cranby watched in disbelief as the half-king was made whole. Finally, healthy skin flowed over nerves, vessels and organs. By some alchemy the left side of his body was joined with the right, leaving no trace of a scar. Before him stood a young man, who smiled gently, before taking a step back and bowing to him.

Fabric rustled as the bearers also knelt to pay obeisance, but not to the new-formed king. To him.

A deep voice emerged from the king. 'The Tears of the Gods are appeased. Take Him.'

Cranby was guided across the chamber and up to the platform. He went slowly, without resistance. There was no fight left in him. If they were going to kill him, he hoped it would be over quickly. He reached the stone throne, and felt its coldness against his back, hips and legs as he was made to sit. His clothes were removed, the gold cloak secured around his shoulders and his hands placed on the stone arms of the throne. A weight settled onto his shoulders and encased his head.

With eyeless sight, he could see through the golden mask. All of them, the young king and the bearers, were standing before him. No one made a move. Perhaps it was over now. Perhaps he could leave. He attempted to raise his hands to the mask to remove it, but nothing happened. His legs too were immoveable. He tried to speak, but his lips seemed frozen.

Help me. Help me, someone. The words echoed in his head, but no one could hear.

Finally, he understood. And then his mind splintered as he realised that he would not die. His body would rot away down to the bones, but he would remain alive and fully conscious. The renewed and new-made man who stood in the chamber was not the king. He was. The Tears of the Gods did indeed grant immortality. This was his kingdom. He reigned over the ruined city in the jungle and would never leave.

Cranby was still screaming in the silence of his mind as the bearers and the past-king went through the door of the vaulted chamber and closed and locked it behind them.

CURIOUS, IF ANYTHING

C.C. Adams

It's not what you look at that matters; it's what you see.
— Henry David Thoreau

Cold linoleum under his feet, Babafemi stood there. Not frightened but curious, if anything. Pale light of early morning crept through the awning window over the bathtub and chased away the last of the bathroom's shadows, and it was *there* in that room of grimy and green chequered tile that, rather than run, Babafemi raised a hand to the tuft of his greying beard, stroking it in contemplation.

Ghost.

Really?

The dark-skinned body in the bathtub lay there, sightless — and had it been a real dead body, Babafemi most likely would have run. Not because he was scared of dead bodies, but more because he'd be scared that someone had left a dead body in his home, and as a result, it would make sense to leave before the killer came back. Assuming, of course, that the killer had left. All of these thoughts fluttered through Babafemi's mind in moments, bringing him back to the present.

The body lying in the bathtub, one leg hanging over the side, the head resting against the side of the hot water tap. A body that he could see through, and despite the darkness of its skin – or at least what would *pass* for skin – he could still see through it: see the outline of the bathtub, the tiling above the tub.

Babafemi already knew it was a ghost since the body was see-through. Unlike many others who may have claimed that they had seen a ghost, or at least felt a ghostly presence, Babafemi was sure that he had encountered supernatural phenomena throughout his years. Early childhood long ago in Nigeria had shown him the ugly side of human nature and desensitised him to death. Later life in London led him to flirt with the supernatural, or certainly with those things that would make others uncomfortable. Time spent in a cemetery at night – back when cemeteries were unlocked and desecration was unheard of – yielded shivers from nothing except freezing cold temperatures among the headstones. Nothing went bump in the night then. Later life (and residences) in London, back when life had led him to adapt to the challenges of marriage, children, divorce and more, had provided more encounters: the sense of being watched by someone or something. Certainly nothing malevolent, but more in the way a curious family pet will watch its human masters before going its own way. And likewise, there was nothing to fear.

But a ghost?

Still stroking his beard, Babafemi folded his other arm

across his chest and took a tentative step closer. The body was of medium height, slim like Babafemi, albeit a little shorter. The foot hanging over the side of the tub was long, and presented a modest bunion. Unsure as to whether he could or should pass through the apparition, Babafemi stopped short of the big toe and braced a hand against the side of the tub as he peered closer, the muscle in his lower back groaning in protest. So much for looking young; some things your body was hopeless at lying about.

The ghost lay in the bathtub.

Unmoving.

A conversation from years ago came back to him, rising like an underwater air bubble to the surface of his consciousness.

'You don't believe in ghosts?' she asked.

'I believe... I believe there are some phenomena, which we may never be fully aware of. But as far as ghosts are concerned, I've never seen one. But I don't think I'd be scared of one. Ghosts are dead, so they can't hurt you. Besides, most times people see a ghost, it's the ghost of someone they know. What do you have to fear from someone you know – especially if they're dead?'

The tentative smile on Janet's face said that while she didn't agree with his logic, she certainly understood it. Admired it, even.

Ghosts couldn't hurt you.

Could you hurt them?

Babafemi's gaze slid up the naked form and settled on the face. A much older face, given the sharper relief of the cheekbones, the sunken cheeks. Eyes cloudy like pearls and devoid of pupils stared straight ahead. Babafemi raised his right hand, holding it over the ghost's shoulder.

One leg still hung over the side of the bath; the body still laid slumped in the bathtub; cloudy eyes still stared straight ahead. All the while, morning nudged back the pale of dawn.

Babafemi brought his hand down onto the apparition's shoulder.

Into the shoulder.

Until it came to rest on the slick hardness of the bathtub itself.

The apparition shimmered.

Vanished.

Many minutes later, Babafemi had climbed into the tub himself, drawn the curtain and run the shower, hot water peppering him as he soaped with slow and pensive movements. His gaze not on the lathering of his body, but the bathtub – always the bathtub.

A busy day in the office followed, then an evening of laps in the pool and now a quiet meal of tuna salad while watching Arsenal play Man City on Sky Sports back at home. Too bad the Gunners were getting their asses handed to them. With the game done, his meal long since reduced to flecks of tuna and dressing smeared across his plate, Babafemi made his way back upstairs and pushed open the bathroom door.

The ghost still laid there, one leg hanging over the tub, its head resting to the side of the hot water tap.

Babafemi hadn't expected anything else, not really.

It had been lying there when he first got in the house. He'd seen it when he went to the bathroom to empty his bladder on returning home.

Again, he approached the tub and leaned over the ghost.

No reaction.

Babafemi's gaze settled on its face. The lips lay parted, no doubt from the once-living person taking their final breath, the eyes staring straight ahead. No change. In other words, normalcy – or at least a sense of normalcy.

It then begged the question: why was it here? It wasn't an omen. Since coming back in the house, Babafemi had already called his brother Wole in Dollis Hill, and his sisters back home. All had confirmed they were safe and sound, apart from Iyabo's texting him after his missed call to ask him what was up, which he took to mean the same thing. So the family were okay. But then, if the family were okay, why did the thing in the bathtub look so familiar? Because it didn't look like any of *them*.

So who…?

He rested the phone against his chin. Tapped the screen against his lips, pondering the idea. Cameras had come a long way since the likes of the old bulky Kodak jobs from the seventies and eighties. *Who? Hmmmm.*

When no answers came, Babafemi hit the camera app on his phone and sized the bathtub in the viewfinder. A click of the button gave a flash of light.

Still no reaction from within the bathtub.

Thumbing through the pictures in the gallery to the latest one, he arrived at a surprisingly clear image of what looked to be a naked black man in a bathtub. *Which is what you would expect*, Babafemi thought; just because it defied conventional explanation, it didn't mean it wasn't there.

He pulled the lid down on the toilet seat and sat, exhaling a slow sigh of contemplation.

So it was nothing to do with his family. What did that leave? Was it something to do with his house? With him?

As far as he knew, he was in good health, considering his age. Some men his age, regardless of race, would have been happy to slide into pudgy middle age, yet at fifty-seven years of age, Babafemi would pass for late thirties, according to most people in the office. For the black acquaintances he had, most pegged him at early-to-mid-forties. A largely pescatarian diet and regular swimming kept him in shape, and apart from a chilled couple of bottles of Bulmers on the weekend, he had no vices to speak of. Still, maybe it would help to pay the GP a visit; err on the side of caution.

That left the house. Babafemi had lived there for a couple of years now, but had always put the easing and creaks within those walls down to subsidence and such. Was it something else at work?

He thumbed open the browser on his phone and brought up the Google homepage and ran a number of searches on the property. Nothing, apart from an obscure reference to Montpelier Road, a good number of streets away from his Altenberg Avenue. *Nothing so strange about this house, anyway*, he thought as he shrugged and looked over his shoulder at the tub.

Still the sightless face lay in profile.

Something crawled wormlike from the back of the head.

Oh.

Ass lifting off the seat, Babafemi craned his neck.

Blood trickled from the back of the ghost's head.

Ohhh…

He pushed to his feet and stepped towards the bathtub to look more closely. While the head and face of the ghost were hazy like the gauze of a fishnet, he couldn't see any wound at the back of the head that the blood would be leaking from. But it was there all the same: a steady viscous trail of red under the apparition's ear that slid over the curved rim of the bathtub and continued an unhurried descent to the bottom of the tub.

But, why now?

For this to happen now suggested something had changed. The only thing that had changed, as far as Babafemi could tell, was that he had taken steps to find out why the ghost was even here. Was that a bad thing?

With a dreamlike slowness, the head slid down the rim. It trailed a smear of blood as it described a slow arc *through* the tap until it came to rest lower down in the tub. From this angle, those sightless pearled eyes stared up at the ceiling.

Babafemi rested a hand on the sink, and bit his lip. Gravity was a real phenomenon (and with every passing day, gravity coupled with age and left Babafemi a shade slower and weaker than before), but this was unnatural. The thing in the bathtub was hardly there; well, not entirely – but it slid down in the tub like a...

dead body.

Maybe that was expected: the exact narrative of the person that gave rise to the ghost. An accident in the bathroom, perhaps someone old and alone, drifting from day to day. Each passing day more hazardous than the last until something as innocuous as splashes of water on the bathroom floor proved disastrous. Eyes filmed with cataracts would miss the spillage, and the person would slip, collapse into the bathtub and hit their head in the process. Life would leak from the body as the blood did, and gravity's pull would *gradually* win out as flesh grew cold and stiff. Oh, yes, tragic circumstances for sure, but what could Babafemi do about…

Slowly, the head began to roll to the side – too slow for this to be the pull of gravity, more like the response to being sworn at in mid-conversation.

A breeze blew through the room, drifting across Babafemi's neck and raising a patch of goose bumps down to his shoulders – a gentle wind…

like someone sighing.

No.

No doubt the expression was the same as it had always been – it was dead, after all – but the expression was aimed in his direction. Sightless eyes, now framed by lowered brows, hooded brows.

Anger?

Of course, Babafemi couldn't avoid thinking who the ghost could possibly be angry with, but as to why? That didn't bear thinking about. As much as Babafemi prided himself on his rationality, the recurring vision in the bathtub began to wear at it, with the slow persistence of time, like wind and rain against rock. Ghosts couldn't hurt you.

You hope.

Go to bed, you old fool. Go to bed.

And with his inner monologue chiding him, he backed out of the bathroom and did just that.

But you're still here. What if it's angry with you?

It's not been angry yet.

Yes, yet. But what if it's angry now?

Why would it be angry with me? Why now?

There, my friend, therein lies the rub.

Apart from the occasional twist or turn, sleep carried

him through to morning without incident. The quiet that settled over the house during the night continued until morning, so much so that when Babafemi slid out of bed to get up for the day, the whisper of his bare feet across carpet seemed loud by comparison. He shuffled to the bathroom, and relieved himself, shaking off at the bowl while he looked over his shoulder at the tub. The empty tub.

Oh.

Babafemi gave a mental shrug as he flushed the cistern. *Nothing lasts forever, not even ghosts, I guess.* Closer inspection of the tub revealed nothing more than a few pubic hairs twisted around the spokes of the plughole. *I guess if they come without trace, they can leave without trace. Unlike these hairs*, he thought wryly.

Babafemi straightened up and turned – faltering.

Head hung low, the ghost hovered in the bathroom's doorway.

So Babafemi stood wary, frowning, lips parted in confusion. So much for the façade of a dead body, this… this was…

Silence pressed in on him, blood thumping in his ears.

The figure glided forward, head still low, until it came within an inch of Babafemi, who took an unconscious step back. Though hazy in appearance, the room's green tiling gleamed through the apparition as it hung in the air like a patient spider on a strand of a web.

It lifted its head, cloudy pearl eyes gazing at him.

Eyes widening as the mouth opened.

Eyebrows now lowered in a scowl as the mouth pulled into an ugly frown, the head shaking to and fro.

And panic stung Babafemi like a barrage of hot needles.

Wind blasted through the bathroom, throwing the door wide open with a splintering of wood. The second blast of air hit Babafemi in the chest, knocking him off his feet and throwing him backward. His calf caught the edge of the tub, tripping him where he fell, smacking his head with terrible force. To Babafemi, it sounded like the crack of a large egg, as if someone were making an omelette, the sound echoing in the confines of his skull as well as vibrating through the tub. Underneath him, cold enamel leached warmth from his bare back, his ass, his leg… The other leg hung over the edge of the tub at an awkward angle. Try as he might, he couldn't generate force or momentum to push out of the tub; the impact alone had fazed him. Something warm trickled down the back of his neck. Consciousness slipping, Babafemi reached a hand to the back of his neck, his fingertips coming away red, slippery red.

Owwww … so stupid … all broken-doll, lying here just like – and *that* was when the realisation washed over him, as if he had slipped beneath the icy surface of a lake. It *was* something to do with the family, but it was with the closest family member of all: Babafemi himself.

His heart thudding in his chest, Babafemi stared at the figure, its open-mouthed horror a reflection of his own. Chills from his skin sunk deeper into him, as the blood continued to ooze its way down the side of his neck. Now the apparition braced one hand next to his prone leg and bent over him, facing him even as the clouded eyes remained rolled up in its head. And as it leaned forward open-mouthed, those eyes widened and one trembling hand lifted and jabbed an accusing forefinger.

Like a master commanding a dog.

CANCER THE CRAB

Lewis Williams

Cancer the Crab hadn't stood a chance. None of them stood much of a chance with him. This fisherman took both claws. Officially, he was only supposed to take one from each crab, but taking both made his life easier and his work quicker and more productive, which kept his boss's accountant happier. And who'd ever catch him? One crab's claw looked pretty much like another. Who could say whether a left and a right claw came from the same or different crabs? He held Cancer's arms apart as the crab's pincers twitched in opening and closing for the last time. Then with a quick and well-practised snap he broke off each of the arms in quick succession before tossing Cancer back in the sea. The whole process took only a few seconds. Did Cancer feel pain? Did Cancer feel stress? Was Cancer so much worse off than if the fisherman had only given him a single declawing and left him with one arm and claw left to communicate with, to fight with, to dig a burrow with, to attract a mate with and to gather food with? His claws were there for a reason, for many reasons. Would it have been better if he'd been kept intact after being caught only to be boiled alive before being eaten. As it was, he would still be living as someone far away enjoyed eating the flesh from his claws.

Studies showed that less than a third of crabs with one claw removed died. Even among those with both claws removed still less than half died. The rest survived, scavenging food. They called it sustainable fishing. Cancer knew nothing of research studies or sustainable fishing, but Cancer *was* a survivor. Every life has its setbacks, and there are those who give up and those that keep on going. Although rarer than the fishermen told themselves it was, it was even possible that Cancer could regrow his arms and claws. Crabs can naturally autotomise, that is self-amputate or shed their own limbs, then about a year later, after a series of moults, regenerate those limbs. Crabs are altogether strange. They walk sideways. They don't even grow as you might expect, but go through a series of moultings where each hard shell is discarded as the crab grows a new one underneath the old, and at the time of the moulting the crab literally climbs out of its own exoskeleton. Nature is stranger than fiction.

Life went on. The days grew shorter and it would soon be Christmas. Each day the fisherman would pack away his things, and as he did so this time he was overcome by a fit of coughing. He'd been troubled by a cough for a few weeks now, a cough that didn't seem to want to go away. Inside his lungs an uncontrolled growth of abnormal cells was beginning to interfere with the normal functioning of his body. A tumour was beginning to grow.

Every life has its setbacks.

WORSE THINGS

Molly Thynes

"The rookies have been calling this the 'reverse eagle'," Detective LeSeur said, pulling a manila folder from his briefcase. "When I first heard it, I thought it was a sex position."

Opening the folder, he threw a stack of photos onto the coffee table. "It's not."

A sour taste crept up Congressman John Wright's throat as he leaned forward to get a closer look. The photos all depicted the same act of violence, each one taken from a different angle, but the photo at the top showed the whole scene. A young woman with pink-dyed hair sat propped up face-first against a lamp post. Her back had been completely torn apart, flayed open like a devoured oyster. Every single one of her ribs had been broken at the spine, each one ragged at the ends and covered in black grimy finger marks. They had all been pulled outwards towards her sides until they resembled a pair of wings. Her lungs had been pulled out through her gaping back and were draped on the ground, covered in debris and coagulated blood. Other of the photos showed that her eyes were left open, wide as though they were still living every horror of the torture she had been put through.

"I had to do a lot of very morbid research for this one," the detective told him. "This was a method of execution favored by the Vikings."

Detective LeSeur leaned back in his chair and stirred the sweet tea that John's wife had brought him just before she left to go Christmas shopping with the kids. The detective and the congressman had been speaking regularly – over the phone and over Skype – for the last two months. Now with the Wright family back in Baton Rouge for the Congressional holiday recess, this was the first time they were meeting face to face.

But the detective was not here to take pictures or speak to the congressman as a constituent. He was here because Congressman John Wright was a person of interest in an ongoing homicide investigation.

Detective LeSeur tapped his fingers against his armrest, waiting for John to respond with something. Eventually, the congressman said, "I don't know this woman."

"Really? Because she knew *you* very well." Detective LeSeur moved the photos aside until he found one that showed a closeup of her face. "She was going to host another rally calling for your resignation this Saturday. I think this would have been her third."

So, that had been little bit of a lie on John's part. He might have never met her in person, but he knew who she was. It was Cat Nelson. She was a grad student – Gendered Native Basket Weaving Studies or something – at Louisiana State University. For the last several weeks, she had called his staff office every single day and had even made it all the way to Washington D.C. to hold a small rally outside the Capitol Building. Her Twitter feed was nothing but calls to celebrities, political leaders, or anyone who would listen: #RacistJohnWright, #John-WrightWhiteSupremacist, #JohnWrightResignNow.

"Well, it's a bit of an occupational hazard," John chuckled. "Being a politician, people are going to disagree with you, and they're going to do it very loudly and very publicly."

"True." Detective LeSeur reached back into his briefcase and retrieved a new folder. "The issue, Congressman, is that all of your opponents are developing a nasty habit of turning up dead at the hands of the same killer."

The detective laid out a row of photos in front of John as a CD of Christmas carols the kids had left on played from the other room: *Carol of bells, sweet silver bells, all seem to say, throw cares away.* They were no gruesome crime scene photos this time, but pictures friends and family had taken of the victims at their happiest.

Yes, *victims.* Cat Nelson was not the first person who had spoken up against the congressman and ended up dying a very gruesome death. She was the fourth.

"Let's go back to the first victim." Detective LeSeur picked up the first photo. "Gordan Nash."

"Right, the YouTuber."

The first photo showed Gordan holding up a goldfish he had won at some street fair. Of course, on YouTube, he was better known as GordyPordy. Most of his channel was just devoted to funny sights and local events around the Baton Rouge area: where to get the best gumbo, which shops had been robbed by naked men on bath salts, and the occasional video showing off a new trick his dog had learned.

"He was the one who brought the scandal to a nationwide audience, wasn't he, Congressman?"

GordyPordy had been a small fish for years, until he created his first viral video. The one where he shared a story about his congressman, John Wright, and how it had been discovered that the biggest contributor to his reelection campaign was Heritage Shield, the white supremacist organization that had been organizing marches all across the state.

"I have to tell you, Congressman, Heritage Shield are not good people to be involved with," the detective said before finally taking his first sip of tea. "They've been keeping my department busy for years. One of their lieutenants is currently awaiting trial for running over a counter-protester with his diesel truck. Not to mention more charges of assault and property destruction than I can count."

"As soon as the story broke, I held a conference denouncing racism in all its forms!"

"Yes, I saw the conference when I watched Gordan Nash's video."

Apparently, the congressman's statements had not been good enough for GordyPordy.

"He said in his video," the detective continued, "that if you were serious, you would publicly denounce Heritage Shield by name, and return any money they contributed to your campaign. And you never did."

"You said it yourself, these are dangerous people."

Not to mention that losing the money that Heritage Shield had contributed would mean losing nearly forty percent of the contributions to his reelection campaign.

But with each passing day that the congressmen did

not comply with GordyPordy's 'demands', the video gained more and more views, and what started as just a local story in the Louisiana capital spread across the country, with mentions on the news every single night.

"Because of Mr. Nash's video, you started having a lot of your local constituents speaking out publicly against you," the detective said, as he picked up another photograph. "Not just Miss Nelson, but people like the Reverend Gellert."

John groaned to himself. Reverend Mark Gellert, in a way, had been worse than all the others combined. With John's mainly conservative base, it was easy enough to write off Gordan Nash or Cat Nelson as crazy liberal socialists, but the good reverend was a 'humble man of God'. At the very first rally against the congressman in Baton Rouge, Reverend Gellert managed to get himself on camera, giving a public sermon, going on about "let no one deceive you with empty words" and "I do not sit with deceitful men, nor will I go with pretenders. I hate the assembly of evildoers, and I will not sit with the wicked."

And then people on both sides began listening, including those residents of the second district who had voted for John Wright. And then those people started calling John's office, wanting to know why he wasn't renouncing Heritage Shield, and saying that their vote depended on it.

John glanced down at the table. The photograph of the good reverend showed him leading the dinner prayer at a local homeless shelter. *What? No pictures of him hugging a refugee or blowing a limbless veteran?*

"It must have been difficult," the detective remarked.

"You won your district by a landslide five years ago. And then to see them all turn against you. All because of these four people right here."

"I would not say they turned against me," John replied. "All politicians have moments in their careers when an issue splits their constituents. A true leader knows how to bring people together, in spite of opposition."

"And did that start getting easier? After the opposers started turning up dead?"

The detective reached into his briefcase again, setting another photo on top of the one of Gordan Nash, one of the photos that had been taken at his crime scene.

On October 9th, a pair of fourth graders on their way to school stumbled across Gordan Nash's body in a park. According to the congressman's sources, the children were still refusing to walk to school, despite weekly visits to a child psychologist.

John's stomach clenched as he stared down at the photo. Gordan Nash's body had been tossed beside a pile of leaves, but no attempt had been made to cover him. Sections of his flesh had been cut away from his chest and sides, muscles exposed and fat spilling out onto the grass. His arms and legs had been amputated, the stubs dangling and the bones exposed. His face was a mass of gaping holes where his ears and nose had been cut away, his mouth stuck in a permanent grin with exposed teeth where his lips had been sliced away. Eventually, the papers identified the method by which he was killed as Lingchi, the Chinese execution method of Death by a Thousand Cuts.

But no one contacted the congressman when Gordan

Nash had been found. The police's initial theory was that the boy had been killed by either a crazed fan or some random weirdo. And that even with as brutal a method of death as this had been, there was no reason to believe the killing was anything other than an isolated incident.

Then, three weeks later, they found the body of Emma Hill, the reporter who had actually broken the story about the congressman's largest campaign contributor. She had been found just outside the newspaper office with her midsection torn open, her innards ripped to shreds. According to the coroner, rat droppings were found inside her abdominal cavity.

That was when the papers started calling the killer the Second District Executioner. That was also when Detective LeSeur first started contacting John's office.

"You know, Detective," John said, "you keep calling me a person of interest in this investigation, but you still have not told me I'm an actual suspect."

Detective LeSeur leaned back in his chair, crossing one leg over the other. "No. Any competent officer could do the most basic research and see you were in DC at the time of these murders."

"And how do you even know that these murders were all committed by the same person?" the congressman then asked. "I'm only a casual viewer of *Criminal Minds*, but don't serial killers tend to use the same sort of method? Or go after the same sort of people."

The detective snorted at the statement, and John cast his eyes down toward the floor. Even he knew that was a weak attempt. Four different killers operating within a twenty-mile radius, going after different victims, who all happened to have been speaking out against the congressman? There wasn't a lawyer with a bottomless case of bribe money who would argue that defense.

"Let's not waste each other's time, Congressman," the detective said bluntly. "I don't actually believe you had anything to do with these murders. I don't think you have the stomach for something this brutal."

On some level, John could have been offended by that statement, but then he realized that he would be defending the statement that he was capable of slicing someone apart piece by piece. Not the sort of thing that one bragged about in a thirty second ad during the Tigers game.

"But I do think you may know more than you think. Whoever is responsible for these murders thinks they're doing it for you. It's no coincidence that they are killing using history's most brutal execution methods. They are going after people they see as traitors to you personally, and they're executing them for their crimes."

The detective got up from his chair and moved to sit on the couch, beside the congressman. "A person going to all this trouble and who believes their cause is righteous is not going to keep this quiet. I wouldn't be shocked if this person tried to contact you personally to gain your approval.

"I'm sure that one of your aides informs you when they receive any disturbing calls or messages. And believe me, if this person ever did try to contact your office, no one would be able to just brush it off and ignore it. They would tell someone."

This was one point that the two men could agree on. This generation was made of so many sensitive little snowflakes, they would come to the congressman crying anytime someone on the phone said something even remotely upsetting. But none of his aides had come to him saying that crazy killers were calling them asking if the lambs had stopped screaming.

John should have told the detective that, but he just sat on the couch, avoiding eye contact. *Defend yourself, dammit!*

Detective LeSeur moved on to a different tactic. "There are a lot of people out there who deserve justice for their loved ones. You might be able to provide them with that."

The detective selected a crime scene photo from those on the table and actually placed it in John's hands. "Reverend Gellert here had an entire church of people who cared about him. Not to mention thousands of others in the community. Don't you think they at least deserve to know why he was taken from them?"

The reverend had been left on the steps of his own church. In the photograph, he lay sprawled out on the steps, staring up at the sky. Burns lined his entire naked body, ripples of deep burns – deep red and black – like zebra stripes, flesh peeling away in blackened curls.

"A poor attempt at grilling," the detective had told John when the body was first discovered, "the same way St. Lawrence was killed."

Was he trying to be ironic with this one? Or is he so dense that this went right over his head?

"I'm sorry, Detective, but I don't have anything new to say," John told Detective LeSeur. "You know everything I know."

Detective LeSeur pursed his lips and took the photo back.

"Tomorrow, the FBI is going to be coming into Baton Rouge to take over the investigation," he reminded the congressman. "Once that happens, I am going to move down to the bottom of the totem pole on this investigation, and there's nothing I can personally do to help you anymore. Do you understand that?"

The detective had been holding this over his head for a couple of weeks: *the FBI are coming; the FBI will be getting involved at some point.* For a long time, it had just been a threat: *Just think what this will do to your reelection campaign* and all that. But apparently four dead bodies were what it finally took for the federal government to get involved.

John rubbed his hands over his face, but then moved back to sit straight up on the couch. "Is there anything else you need before you go?"

Detective LeSeur made no movement to get up. Yes, there was indeed something else. "I'm curious why you have not asked me anything about your campaign manager, Joseph Walden."

"*Former* campaign manager," the congressman corrected. "Joe and I broke ties months ago."

"Yes, I've been seeing his campaign volunteers out on the streets."

It was barely a week after the scandal broke that Joe had announced, without even the curtesy of telling John first, his candidacy against him in next year's primary. In his announcement, Joe had told the second district that "he felt responsible for unleashing John Wright on Washington" and was taking responsibility for it by running for Congress himself, so he could set it all right.

"He's still missing, in case you were wondering," the detective informed him. "Five days now."

The night John and his family arrived back in Baton Rouge for the Congressional recess, Joe's disappearance was all that was talked about on the evening news. Of course, as a new political candidate, Joe was a very public figure. And with all of John's 'enemies' turning up dead in graphic ways, the police had made the case the department's top priority case. John was actually amazed there were no reporters crowding outside his gates at this very moment.

"You're sure you've heard nothing from him?" Detective LeSeur asked. "He hasn't contacted you in any way?"

"I don't know why he would." John set his drink down with a small thud of emphasis.

John and Joe had not even spoken since the night Joe had announced his candidacy. There had been no fight, no shouting matches over the phone. They just cut their ties with one another without saying a single word to each other.

"Well, if you do hear from him, you have my card. Please contact me directly. You know his wife has been in hysterics."

Poor Dora. She was a sweet thing. Always brought a plate of cookies to the house for when John and his family arrived home for Christmas. There had been no plate waiting for them when they arrived home this year.

"Have a good evening, Congressman," the detective said as he finally got up to show himself to the door. "Merry Christmas."

Once the detective had gone and with the door firmly shut behind him, John was left alone in the empty house. The Christmas CD had ended at some point during the conversation, and the house had gone quiet. Leah and the kids would probably still be out for at least another hour.

After spending a good minute and a half tapping his fingers on his knees, John finally forced himself to stand, and went up the staircase, to the second door on the right that served as his office. It contained a desk and a few paintings from Bed Bath & Beyond, but there was nothing personal adorning the space. Since his election, the family spent so little time in their old house that coming back to it now was more like living in a hotel than a home. The kids never even had enough time to leave their rooms a mess.

The congressman settled in the leather rolling chair and turned on the computer monitor. The Skype window was open, and there were ten missed calls from the last two hours.

John had just barely processed the information on the screen when the Skype ringtone began going off again. He didn't want to, but he reached over for the mouse and answered the call.

The screen opened to a young man, not a day older than twenty. He stood out in the middle of the woods, his clothes and hair both half-drenched and caked in mud, and the fuzzy picture telling just how far away he was from the nearest cell tower.

"Congressman, where were you?"

"I'm sorry," John sighed. "Even when I'm on break, I'm not really on break. It's the life of a politician."

"That's okay, Congressman. I know your work is really important."

The young man had been in contact with the congressman since mid-October, insisting he was a constituent, and that he *would have* voted for the congressman, but had been too young for the last election. John had no idea what the young man's name was, and frankly, he did not want to know.

"But I just thought you would really want to see this."

The camera moved away from the boy's face and down towards the ground as he began climbing over fallen trees and forest debris. The further he moved into the wilderness, the damper the ground became; an audible *squelch* could be heard with every step as the forest turned to swamp. Spanish moss draped and trailed into the algae-laced water-bodies that were becoming closer and larger.

"Here we are!"

The boy lifted his phone to show what was in front of him out in the bayou. Two wooden crates bobbed in the swamp with holes cut in the side; arms and legs and a head dangled from the holes. The man was barely conscious, his head slumping, and a long piece of plastic tubing protruding from his mouth. But John knew who it was.

Joe Walden.

"It's called The Boats," the young man proclaimed. "The Persians used to use it. You're supposed to nail the person inside two boats and send them out into a stagnant pond."

The boy then moved the phone so that it was facing him again, capturing how wide he smiled despite his heavy breathing from the hike. "I didn't have two boats laying around, sadly, but at least we have plenty of swampland."

John's shoulders slumped and he sunk into his chair. The Second District Executioner had found a fifth traitor and was in the process of punishing him for his crimes, and he wanted John to watch. Just like John had watched most of the other killings.

He did not witness the death of Gordan Nash, but the day after his body was discovered, the killer contacted the congressman on his direct phoneline to let John know he was the one who did it. During the first contact, John had just hung up the phone, thinking it was a prank call. Ever since the scandal broke, his office had been receiving a lot of those. But then the killer somehow got a hold of the congressman's private Skype account. And he decided he would prove to the congressman how devoted he was to his cause by executing Emma Hill right there on the screen.

In the call, he had tied the young woman down to a rack of some sort with a gag in her mouth. There was a metal bucket strapped to her abdomen and it was moving and squeaking. The boy placed heated coils on top of the bucket. One, then two, then four, until the bucket began shaking violently and Emma Hill shrieked through the gag and blood ran between her skin and the lip of the bucket.

After ten minutes, after Emma Hill finally stopped moving and stopped screaming, the young man came and lifted the bucket away. Emma's entire abdomen had been torn away, with her stomach and intestines exposed, the rats swimming in the cavity, covered in blood.

And then he called the congressman back again, so he could watch the execution of Reverend Mark Gellert. And then Cat Nelson's.

The young man smacked Joe in the side of the head. "Mr. Walden, it's time to wake up."

Joe jolted awake, and immediately began babbling and writhing back and forth in the crate, but his voice was garbled, unable to make proper words with the length of tubing going down his throat.

"He's not going to be able to say very much to you," the boy explained. "They usually become delirious after three days."

The boy set the phone up on the crate, propped up so John could still see him as he rummaged through his sack before extracting a gallon jug of pale gold liquid.

"You have to feed them more milk and honey every day," he explained. "It keeps them from dying too quick, and it provides more food for the insects."

The young man picked up the end of the plastic tubing and began pouring the liquid down Joe's throat. At first, Joe didn't seem like he even knew anything was happening, but as the bottle got closer to empty, Joe began to writhe and groan inside the crate. Was it even possible for a human being to consume that much liquid in one sitting?

"The Persians would reserve this method of execution for the very worst traitors that society had to offer," the boy explained as he continued to pour. "And that's exactly why I chose it. This was your right-hand man, the person you trusted more than any other with your political career, and he went around your back to usurp you. He deserves nothing less."

Finally, there was no more left, and the young man began squeezing the tubing, forcing the last few drops into Joe's stomach.

"I'll come back tomorrow and do it again. The bugs

just started coming around here, and hopefully by tomorrow, there will be a lot more."

Along the edges of the crate, a collection of flies, hornets, and other assorted winged things were making the way in and out of the holes. They had made themselves comfortable, resting on Joe's skin, red, bloated, and blistered from welted bites and stings.

"I can't tell if any of them have started laying eggs in his skin yet, but I don't want to open the crates and let them all out."

The young man picked up the phone again and smiled, waving at the camera. "Have a good night, Congressman. I'll call you tomorrow so you can see how it's going."

The Skype screen went black, and the congressman sat frozen in his chair. Detective LeSeur's card was still in his desk drawer. He could pick up the phone right now, give a perfect description of the Second District Executioner, and even give them the name of his Skype account. There had to be some way to trace him through that. And the longer John waited, the worse this was going to be for him. By not going to the police, he was guilty of conspiring or enabling, and the crimes were horrific enough that he might end up getting the needle along with the kid.

John reached into his desk drawer and extracted Detective LeSeur's card.

But if the kid was caught – because John called the detective or because the kid eventually made a mistake – John's political career was over. His *life* would be over, through no fault of his own. The only way John would be staying in office is if the police just never found out this kid in the backwoods of Louisiana was killing all of John's enemies. They never caught the Zodiac Killer. There was a chance it could happen.

And in the meantime, it had been two weeks since the news had been reporting anything about Heritage Shield. And now, thanks to some insects and honey, he would be running completely unopposed in the upcoming primary.

John traced his fingertips over the sharp edges of the card, flipping it over in his fingers.

There could be worse things.

John tossed the detective's card back into the open desk drawer and smiled, unable to help himself.

BELIEVE AND BE JUSTIFIED

Felix Flynn

I am one of the faithful.

No ropes had been needed to bind me, no chains or shackles required to keep me tethered. My convictions had held me in place on that carved stone altar, cold against my fevered skin.

Once I had been chosen, they had washed me. The other worshippers joined me in the oversized bath that resided in the inner sanctum of our chapel. Any one of the congregation would have given anything to be in my place, to be granted the same promise that had been given to me and others before me: paradise. I saw the envy in their eyes as they poured warm water over my skin, rubbed my limbs, my chest, my back, with rosemary and thyme. Oils were massaged into my flesh, leaving it gleaming in the flickering glow of the torches around us. I recall closing my eyes and breathing deeply, dragging the fragrances of the herbs and sweet oils into my lungs. I could feel Him in each breath I took, in each touch on my skin, in the water, in the very air. The temple was filled with His presence.

Feeling Him in the air was like static on my skin or a warm embrace. He was energy and peace, damnation and salvation all in one. He was there for me, watching me become worthy.

I had to wait as my brothers and sisters stepped out of the water to circle me. They joined hands and their voices rose into a chant of prayer. It moved me, shook me to my core. Their love, *His* love, was enough to bring me to tears and leave me dizzy.

Though perhaps that was simply the effect of the heat of the water, which at that moment felt almost too hot. I knew it wasn't. It was Him, His glory gripping me, leaving my mind foggy as I started to sweat.

Once prepared, I was taken out through the back door and into the woods behind the chapel. The Shepard, our earthly leader, led the way.

I was so keenly aware of my surroundings. The wind ghosted through the branches overhead, making the leaves whisper to me. An owl called out somewhere to my right. Moonlight reached down in bright blue beams, caressing my still bare skin. Leaves and twigs covered the path we took, crunching and snapping beneath my heels. They should have hurt. I should have winced at each pebble I stepped on, but they didn't cause me pain. I was too giddy at the idea of what was to come.

We stopped at a deep hole, the edge of which was surrounded by old stone. It was all that was left of the ruins our order used to occupy.

The circular stone steps that led us down into the pit seemed to go on forever and each one was taken on shaking legs. I felt dizzy, but I pushed on despite nearly falling twice. I had to stop now and again to brace my hand against the wall to keep from tipping over as my head swam. The others halted when I did, watching and waiting silently. If I fell they wouldn't stop me; I'd go tumbling forward until I hit the landing at the bottom where I would be left, broken, to rot. I'd be deemed unworthy of His grace.

This thought alone urged me forward. Our Lord held me upright. *He* kept me going.

Eventually, the steps led us into a large chamber, lit by candlelight, where the altar stood.

They chanted again after I was placed on the altar, their voices rising and reverberating around me as they sang, filling the vast vacant space with the sound. This would be the last time I saw them in this world. Of course, we would all be together again, once they too joined Him, but for now, this was goodbye. We were a family, a family that loved each other so deeply we knew how necessary it was to leave this place, this diseased world. They understood me as I understood them. Not like the family I had left behind. My mother, father, and sisters hadn't been convinced when I told them that they needed to come with me. They wept, told me to stay, told me that they cared. They didn't. They were just as lost as the rest.

A lost world made of concrete and steel, dying away. Civilization as we knew it was spiraling down a destructive path, trapping us on a planet with dwindling resources, where plants and animals were dying, where we spent our lives in front of screens. We had forgotten the old ways, the Shepard had said when he'd found me. We were all damned, but the willing could be saved. He wanted me to be one of his flock, to earn my place and be delivered from this world to somewhere better.

Now it was my time. I had finally made it.

The hymn the congregation sang wasn't sad, though it sounded melancholy; it was uplifting, reminding me of who we were – the truest believers – and of everything I stood to gain through this.

It was the best parting gift I could have asked for, to be so warm, so filled with their admiration.

They turned away after their harmonized voices finally quieted and started for the stairs. The resounding echoes of their voices were all that they left behind. Their absence gave me a chance to look around this sacred place.

The walls were etched with aged ancient carvings that were no doubt as old as He was. Most of the writings were unreadable, engraved in some script long lost to time. The rest were images, something like hieroglyphs but with a druidic aesthetic. I had to stand on my toes to get a better look at them, but even then they reached too high for me to see them in their entirety.

The drawings depicted the rituals that my peers and I followed, depicted the cleansing, the offering, then paradise.

In front of me loomed an impossibly large open archway that looked as if it'd been unevenly dug into the stone. Perhaps it was a cave and the ritual site had been built around it; except the opening didn't look natural. There were scrapes and scratches etched around the gaping maw as if something had dug its way through, scraped and clawed its way out. The cavern was where He dwelt, I knew.

Something stirred in the inky black of that archway and for a moment I was sure the movement was the dark itself, come alive and threatening to break past the doorway, to flood out onto the floor and eat up the space between us.

It didn't.

My heart picked up its pace, not from fear but excitement, as twin iridescent orbs appeared. Each were as big as my head and from where they seemed to hover, fifteen or so feet up, I could see them glint in the waning candlelight.

Finally.

Finally.

I would become one with my brothers and sisters, my family and friends. One with *Him*.

He came forward into the light, one giant taloned paw at a time. Nails scraped against hard stone. The sound of a heavy body dragging its way closer reached my ears. He was too large for the candles to illuminate completely, but what the glow could reach shined, glossy and wet, with a rainbowed sheen that reminded me of an oil slick. I could make out yellowed tusks, chipped but sharp, on either side of the mouth that was suddenly stretching wide to let out an ear-piercing shriek. He had endless rows of pointed teeth, a purple-blue tongue that swiped out across one of His tusks as the keening cry ended, leaving the bone slippery with thick saliva.

He was beautiful.

Glorious.

Unlike anything I could have imagined. The scripture didn't do Him justice. There were, in the Order's Holy Books, vague pictures of what our Lord looked like, drawn ages ago in the same style that marked the walls around me. I had mused with my brothers and sisters about what He would be like. Would He speak to us?

Would He be silent as He took us to the next life? Would He be kind and loving when confronted with our devotion? The conversations always left us giddy, dreaming of when we would be chosen.

Even my wildest dreams couldn't have prepared me for this.

He was huge, taking up the space of the already enormous chamber, and so real. He was real. *All of this* was real. Not that I had ever doubted Him. A lesser believer might have; they may have been shocked at what they were seeing, but *I* wasn't. Still, I was finding it hard to breathe, I was shaking, and it was difficult to stand any longer. I dropped to my knees before Him.

I imagined what would come next. The Holy Book depicted wonderful light, celebration, and going home to Him, back to where we truly belong. It would be mine now.

A low rumbling growl reverberated from His throat. I did not tremble, even as the altar room around me did. I was not afraid; I had been waiting for this. I wouldn't run from Him, from this, not now, not when I would finally be granted salvation. He had chosen me – *me* – and this was His will.

The candles burned lower, nearly snuffed out, and in the growing darkness He moved closer to bend over me. I could vaguely make out spines rising up out of His ridged back and casting hill-like high shadows against the wall. His head, coming nearer, looked feline in shape, though there wasn't an inch of fur on His smooth skin. Slit nostrils flared as He breathed in my scent. My smell was mixed with – or perhaps masked by – the aroma of the oils and herbs from the bath.

He seemed pleased, which only helped calm me. Our Lord would come in the form of a great beast, tame and sweet, to lead us to our next life; that was what the Shepherd said whenever another of the flock was chosen. The Holy Book told us this. It was why I did not hesitate to reach up and touch His face. My hand ran along His massive jaw, along His flat wet skin. It was sticky, coated in a mucus that clung to my palm and no doubt accounted for the sheen I had seen earlier. I should have been afraid, but I wouldn't allow myself to be. This was right. Everything about this was just as it had been foretold.

Still, my hot skin was turning cold and my mouth had gone dry.

I swallowed hard.

His body went stone still, eyes staring at me unseeing, and it struck me that He was blind. Of course. What need were eyes when finding the hereafter? I was about to close my own in this quiet perfect moment, only He lifted His head some, drawing my attention.

"My Lord," I whispered, breathless in my awe of Him. "My Lord, show me paradise."

My savior opened His maw and I was confronted with those teeth, those razor sharp points perfectly lining dark black gums.

The next few moments were a blur.

With a snarl, He abruptly bit down on my still outstretched arm and jerked me off the altar hard enough to pop my shoulder bone clean out of its socket. I could not register what had happened, even as I was dangling above feet of open air and the floor below. Then it hit me; white hot pain slammed into me and I screamed.

Blood was pouring from His lips down past my elbow to drip onto my throat. It was warm and wet, mixing with the creature's – not creature, *His* – drool. I felt faint. Why was this happening? Was I not worthy? Had He forsaken me? Was I, His most devout, being denied paradise?

No.

No!

I refused to believe it. This was another test, a test of my faith. It only made sense that pain would be suffered, that it needed to be endured, that the pathway to paradise would be found through blood spilled. There had been nothing about this in the Holy Book. But I knew. This *was* a test.

I clamped my mouth shut, refusing to scream again and give Him any reason to deny me.

I could prove my commitment.

I was taken through the archway He had emerged from and was blanketed in the cool dark. Adrenaline pumped through my veins, made me feel sick, and I fought down bile as my arm throbbed from my crushed wrist still caught in His teeth. Agonizing heat pulsed through me. I had *faith*. All of these years of worship and prayer, of study and devotion, it hadn't all been for nothing. And I endured, and I stayed quiet, muffling whimpers at each jarring step He took. Even when He flung me hard against the ground I did no more than stifle a whimper as the wind was knocked out of me and, I was sure, one of my ribs broke. Pain would be payment, I reasoned.

This human coil would be shed soon enough.

Then I would be wrapped in His brilliance and warmth. This was His plan.

The ground beneath me was hard and uneven. As His hot breath washed over me again, my fingers sought for purchase so I could sit up. I wanted to proclaim my devotion to Him, to tell Him of my faith, but the words died in my throat. It wasn't stone under my palms but chipped and cracked bone that covered the floor. Though I couldn't see, I knew it with a cold certainty as my fingertips dipped into a skull's eye sockets, skittered away then slid over a clean rib cage. My breath caught in my throat and was forced out in a cry as His mouth clamped down onto one of my legs. Surely He would forgive me my weakness. I was only human.

His teeth dug into the tender flesh of my thigh, grinding saw-like to rip through meat and bone. It brought a wet crunching sound to my ears as a fresh wave of pain hit me. He was eating me, *eating* me as He'd eaten so many others. It was unbearable, but I *had* to bear it. Tears streaked down my cheeks at the realization.

He was perfect, my magnificent Lord, and I was so lucky He had picked me. I would not give in to doubts. Not now. Not ever.

My other leg was devoured in pulpy juicy bites, His horribly powerful jaws reached my hips, and my grip on the world around me was starting to slip as the agony of it, of His consuming me, became too much. I tasted blood on my tongue, coughed it onto my lips as He began tearing into my stomach, and I smiled. Through the pain, the subtle jerks of my body as He tugged and pulled at my meat, as I was dragged deeper into that awful mouth of His, I saw the truth.

He would tear me up and swallow me down, but my faith told me this wouldn't be the end. I would have my paradise and He was setting me free, inch by inch. I was *happy* for it.

Overjoyed.

THE HAUNTING OF APRIL HEIGHTS

Tricia Lowther

I should've listened to the dog. When I first tried to go through the front door of my new flat, my Airedale cross-breed, Maddy, pulled me back. She nearly yanked my arm off. I rubbed my shoulder. 'What's the matter, girl? Never known you not to stick by my side.'

Fair enough, the hallway was unwelcoming. All the doors were closed, so it was dark. I ordered Maddy to stay, and went inside to let in some light. Three bedrooms ran along the left-hand-side of the corridor and, at the end, another door led to the large living room with its coffin-sized balcony. A door on the far side of the living room led to the kitchen and bathroom. I opened the bedroom and living room doors wide, let the grey daylight in, and called Maddy. Nope. Stubborn creature. There was a half-chewed tennis ball in my bag. I grabbed it and threw it down the hall, shouting, 'Fetch! Come on, girl!' She plonked herself down with a whine, so I shrugged and left her there.

I needed to get on with pre-move cleaning. Maddy's behaviour was weird, but she'd come round, I was sure. Back then, I prided myself on being logical and down-to-earth.

It was the late 1980s on a Liverpool council estate with three high rise blocks named April, May and June Heights. They had a bad reputation: drugs, crime and general squalor – but they were big and cheap. My place was on the top floor of April. It had an amazing view across the city, plus my best mate, Joolz, lived next door. I couldn't afford the rent on my old place since I'd kicked out my constantly stoned and occasionally violent ex. This was my fresh start.

Next time I visited, Joolz was home. She looked after Maddy while I slapped dingy plum paint over the living room walls, Siouxsie and the Banshees for company on the ghetto blaster. The colour had looked warm and interesting in the shop, but in here it seemed to absorb all light. I stepped back, hands on hips, and sighed. The walls emanated gloom. I'd try and brighten the place up later, once I got all my gear in.

On moving day I had to bribe Maddy in. I bought a pig's ear from the market – her favourite. In the van on the way over she drooled at the scent. Once there, I walked down the hallway holding it out and she scuttled in after me, ears flat, tail between legs. Success! She settled down in the kitchen with her reward, and I stuck the kettle on.

Joolz hovered around, sticking her peroxide blonde head in and out of cupboards, commenting on the differences between my place and hers. Mine was better, apparently. 'You could have some brill parties up here, Elise. All this space! I wish we had three bedrooms.' Joolz shared a one-bedroomed flat with her boyfriend, Rob, their whippet, Wraith, and three cats, Mog 1, Mog 2 and Mog 3. At least, that's what I called them. She went on, 'I won't be so bothered by the noises now I know you're in here.'

I squished a teabag on the side of the mug and plopped it in the sink. 'Noises?'

'Yeah. Weird noises at night. They echo through the flats. It's hard to tell where they're coming from exactly. Some nights—' She took a drag on her ciggie, the end stained purple with her lipstick, then continued, 'I'd swear there was someone in here.'

'Right. Thanks for telling me that.' I pulled a face, but I wasn't concerned. Old buildings make noise, so what?

Joolz was a hard-core goth. The music and the make-up appealed to me, but she was into everything: horror films, ghost stories, fortune telling. The idea of my flat being haunted clearly amused her, but I wasn't going to entertain her on it. I pointed to the object by the balcony and grinned. 'Thanks for that, by the way. It's brill. I'll leave the decision of which of my sad, neglected houseplants to put in it until later.'

Her flat-warming gift to me was a huge plant pot. Black, of course, splatted with red squiggles.

Joolz rubbed her arms. 'Tell you what, you need to get a decent heater in here. It's bloody freezing!'

It was late by the time I got around to sorting my bedroom out. I was folding T-shirts to the sound of The Cure when something made me turn the volume down. From the corridor, Maddy growled.

Something in my abdomen shifted, and I searched for a weapon. The pitch of Maddy's growls rose higher and she began to whine. There was a crash, and Maddy's barks grew frenzied. I grabbed my chunky marble ashtray and edged into the hallway.

Cold silence. Then, Maddy hared toward me with frantic little yips. I grabbed her collar and peeped into the living room. The balcony doors were wide open. The floor was a mess. My new plant pot was smashed to pieces. I walked in, picked up a fragment and examined it. Then, I looked over the balcony rail to the pavement, fifteen floors below. No way anyone could have climbed up here. Maddy must have broken the pot, somehow.

'What was it, Maddy? Did you see a bird? Not a rat I hope.'

She gave a low growl.

'What's the matter with you? You've never growled at me before!'

I found the dustpan and brush and swept up the mess while Maddy watched, head tilted to one side. *I won't cry on my first night*, I told myself. It didn't matter. It was just a flowerpot, and Maddy was just unsettled by the move. I pulled the balcony door shut with a shiver, making sure to lock it.

In bed at last, Maddy curled up on the end of my new striped duvet cover, and I ruffled her scruffy black and tan head. No doubt she'd work her way up the bed overnight, try and take it over. Since the break-up I'd found it comforting to have her near at night. The sound of her breathing and little doggy sighs made me feel less alone.

In the night, her growling woke me.

'Sshh, it's okay,' I murmured, thinking she was dreaming, but she lifted her head and stiffened. I squinted at the alarm clock: 2:53am. Maddy was trembling. Her nervy whines grew louder and turned to insistent little barks. Then she sat bolt upright and decided to go for it, full pelt.

'Jesus, Maddy, what is it?!'

I turned the light on, my stomach churning like a washing machine as I checked around the flat. Nothing. But Maddy continued to bark. I did my best to calm her. Eventually, after a few shaky whimpers, she settled down. I found my chunky ashtray and lit a cigarette – 'So much for cutting down on the fags.'

Within a few days, Joolz and I got into the routine of taking our dogs out for a morning walk together on the local field.

'Were you throwing toys for Maddy in the middle of the night?'

'Why would I do that?'

'Well, whatever you were doing kept me awake. All the scuffling noises. It sounded like someone was running up and down your hallway.'

I stopped walking and turned to face her. 'Are you making this up to freak me out, Joolz?'

'No! I—'

'Because if you are, it's not funny! Maddy's been going berserk every bloody night and it's driving me mad! I could do without anything else!'

She shook her head. 'Elise, I'm not making it up, honest. Look, maybe it was someone downstairs. I told you I sometimes hear odd noises. Or maybe it was Maddy in the hallway, playing with a toy by herself.'

'Maddy sleeps in my room. She wakes up barking at exactly seven minutes to three every night.'

One of Joolz's thinly-drawn black eyebrows rose

behind her crimped fringe. 'Maybe that's just the time someone in the building gets home from work?'

'Always at 2:53?'

Joolz shrugged. 'Maybe someone's central heating clicks on at that time?'

'Mmm, maybe. Strange time to set the heating off, though, and I don't see why that would send Maddy berserk. Oi! Maddy!' I staggered as Maddy charged through my legs.

Joolz laughed. 'Yes, because she's normally so well behaved!'

I groaned. Maddy had spotted a game of football in the distance. 'Maddy! Heel!' I tried my most authoritative tone of voice, to no effect. I'd have to apologise to the players once I caught her. She loved to chase balls, and if she spotted one before I could slip her lead on, that was it. Zoom. Dog gone.

Back in the lobby, we bumped into baldy Bill, the caretaker. As he left the lift, I remembered something.

'Bill, I have some letters for the previous tenant. Do you have a forwarding address?'

He hesitated and rubbed at his ear. 'Just pop them into the office. I'll sort it out.'

A scratchy voice like dead leaves came from behind him.

'If it's for Mrs Morgan, write "deceased" on the envelope and send it back.'

A craggy-faced woman, layered in long skirts, coat and shawl shuffled out of the lift. Joolz wrinkled her nose.

The woman pointed at me. 'What's with all the carry on in the middle of the night?'

'I, er…'

'And shut that damned dog up! Don't know what they were thinking when they let you in!' She wandered away, muttering. Maddy threw a defiant bark at her back.

That night, Joolz and Rob were going to a party that I had no desire to attend. My ex would be there, with his new woman. By eight, I was curled up in my huge grey armchair. It was old but comfy. Dad had showed up with it one day, saying they'd only been going to throw it out anyway so I may as well have it. Mum and Dad had been dead set against me moving in with *him* in the first place, so there was no way was I going crawling back to them now. I was fine. I had chocolate, a bottle of Merrydown Cider and 20 Embassy. I had a faithful hound, a VHS collection, and possibly a ghost, but I wasn't going to think about that.

It got cold, so I brought my duvet into the living room and snuggled up in front of the TV. Maddy attempted to get under the duvet with me, but eventually ended up outside it flopped across my legs. Her warm body soothed me. I ran my fingers through her fur and talked to her about my ex, my parents and my skintness. She was such a good listener. By the early hours, I was watching a Kate Bush video, the one where a masked man shadows her every move. That was when something scraped at the living room door. I turned the sound off. Another scrape. Under the duvet, my blood chilled.

Maddy grew taut. She jumped off my lap and faced the door, hackles up. Little puffs of icy air rose from her nostrils. She snarled, long and low. The air filled with static. I wanted to run, but there was nowhere to go. Maddy backed toward me, growling fiercely. Then, she jumped. She snapped at the air. My chest tightened. Then,

Maddy charged towards the balcony and hurled herself at the glass doors.

I let go of the duvet. I'd been clutching it so tightly that my fingers hurt. An odd smell licked at my nose, like a struck match. Maddy whined and scrabbled at the balcony door. 'It's okay, Maddy.' I cuddled her, rubbed and soothed the thick fur around her neck until she calmed down enough to give my face a few stinky, dog-breath licks.

By morning, I'd convinced myself that it had just been a few creaks. Just some of those noises old buildings make. Rats at worst. I was getting freaked out by trivial things because I was on my own. Maddy was sensitive to my feelings. The heating system was ancient. That was why it was always freezing. Everything was explainable. Bad dreams were just bad dreams.

It was a day or two later when I caught up with the old woman from the lift. I spotted her on the road heading back from the newsagents. She was making a painful show of lugging four carrier bags home.

'Would you like some help?' I asked, as she stopped to rub her fingers. She grimaced, which I took as a yes, and I picked up the bags, which were full of tins. By the time we reached the lifts I was glad to drop the bastards. Amidst the scent of ammonia, I asked a stupid question, 'So, what happened to the woman before me?'

She narrowed her beady eyes. 'Went over the balcony.'

After that, every time I ventured onto the balcony, I couldn't help but look down and imagine how Mrs Morgan's body had looked after it hit the ground.

Depression pawed at me. I dreaded winter. It was freezing up here already. The heating didn't work properly, but the guy the council sent round insisted there was nothing wrong with it. I kept music or the television on constantly, but nothing lifted the atmosphere. Only Maddy. She made sure I got up in the mornings.

Some nights I'd wake and think someone was in the room. My breath frosted the air as Maddy's tense growls echoed. One night I woke sure something had clutched my leg. Another night I woke with the sensation of cold hands around my throat. *Just vivid dreams,* I told myself, *just anxiety.*

Thoughts of Mrs Morgan gnawed at me.

One evening, Joolz brought a psychic round. These days everyone's heard of 'The Flamboyant Clairvoyant', Vince Kinsella, but back then he was just Vinny – an old mate of Rob's who told fortunes at parties. Joolz had told him my flat had a strange atmosphere and that I was having bad dreams.

'I've brought Vinny to do an exorcism,' was how she put it when I opened the door.

Vince Kinsella was a skinny goth, white-faced with crimped black hair. He wore a long coat and pointy buckled shoes. He was nothing like the smart-suited, silver-haired guy who now makes appearances on the Ghostly channel, tours theatres, and predicts the future in spooky true-life mags. I was sceptical, but made us all tea and passed the custard creams around. I relayed what old Joan downstairs had told me about the previous tenant. Mrs Morgan had unexpectedly discharged herself from a psychiatric ward, walked home in the middle of the night, and found her husband in bed with someone else. She had then ran screaming through the flat and jumped off the balcony.

Vincent thought that explained things. 'If you feel her presence, tell her to go to the light. Say it clearly and firmly. I doubt she means you any harm.'

At my raised eyebrow, he sighed and put his tea down on the upturned tea chest I used as a coffee table. 'I'll see what I can pick up. Could you lower the lights in here please?'

I lit some candles, put one on the tea chest and two on the mantel piece. As I was about to switch the overhead light off, the temperature dipped and Vincent turned as grey as the armchair he sat in. I'd heard that people's faces can change colour in an instant, but I'd never seen it happen before.

He rasped, 'I have to go,' and that was it. He left.

His tea was still hot.

Joolz ran after him.

'Good job I've got you for company, eh Maddy?' I muttered as we settled down in front of the telly yet again. She dropped her chin onto my knee and gave an offended whine.

It had been hard to get tenancy of this flat. I imagined the look on the council official's face if I asked to be rehoused due to a haunting.

Moving back in with my parents wasn't feasible. Even if I could put up with their smug 'I-told-you-so' looks, they'd never put up with Maddy's moulting. They were extremely house-proud.

Next day, I collected some photos from the chemists. The camera had been lying around in my room and I'd noticed the film had been used up. I couldn't remember what half of them were, probably pics taken on nights out: me, Joolz, Rob and assorted others. There might be some of the ex on there too. I decided to drop in on Joolz. We could look at them together, and maybe she could tell me what had freaked Vinny out so much.

In her kitchen, she made us coffee. 'Vinny saw something. He didn't want to say what, in front of you. He didn't want to frighten you.'

'Oh great. What was it?'

She scrunched her mouth up and looked at her mug.

'Are you enjoying this? Come on Joolz, spill the beans. I have to live there.'

'He said he saw a woman run past. Said she was being chased.'

I frowned. 'The ghost of Mrs Morgan, I suppose? Who was chasing her? Her husband?'

'No.' Joolz chewed her lip. 'He said he wasn't sure it was even human. He said it was old.' She lowered her voice to a whisper. 'Ancient. He said he's never seen anything like it. He was terrified.'

I stayed in Joolz's flat for the rest of the day. Apart from a quick walk, Maddy got left on her own because of her tendency to hassle Joolz's cats. I scoured the 'for rent' section of the local paper. Everywhere was either too expensive or wouldn't allow pets.

Day turned to evening; evening turned to night. 'You can stay here tonight if you want, you know,' Joolz offered with a yawn. 'Kip on the sofa.'

Next door, Maddy barked. 'Thanks, but it's alright. I've left Maddy on her own long enough. I'd best get back. It'll be okay.' Not sure who I was trying to convince. I picked up my bag.

'Oh I forgot! Photos!' I pulled them out and waved them at her with a grin. We went through them, laughing and exclaiming. Then, Joolz stopped. She frowned and stared at me, mouth open.

'What's this?' She handed me the picture. It was dark, so I'd skimmed past it thinking it was underexposed. There were a few that hadn't developed properly.

It was me. Asleep in bed, under my new duvet.

'How...?' The words stuck in my throat. Air pressed in on me. 'I can't go back, Joolz. I can't go back in there.'

Joolz put her hand on my shoulder. 'It's okay, you don't need to. When Rob gets back we'll send him next door for Maddy. You can both stay here tonight. We'll sort something out.'

Nodding, I sniffed and wiped my nose on my hand. Wraith the whippet appeared at my side, whimpered and licked my hand.

Maddy barked again. Rob worked in a city centre pub. He wouldn't be back until after midnight.

'I should go and fetch her. I'll just grab her and come straight back,' I told the paler than usual Joolz.

She stood with me by my front door. I took a deep breath before turning the key. When it opened, there was that weird smell again, sulphurous, like matches.

'Maddy?'

The end bedroom door that faced the front door, the one I always kept shut tight because the flat was so draughty, was wide open. I ran down the hall to the living room. Joolz shouted after me.

'Maddy! Where are you?' I had to get out. I needed air. Icy fingers wrapped around my throat. I clutched my neck. The balcony door was open. I ran through it. Maddy appeared next to me, barking madly.

I clung onto the rail and gulped in cool breathfuls of

air. Every detail of what happened next has remained clear in my mind ever since.

Something shoved me, hard, in the back. If the rail had been any lower, or if I hadn't been holding it so tightly, I'd have gone over. Something rolled up the ridges of my spine. Pressure on the back of my neck pushed my head forward. I stared down at the ground.

Fighting it, I pulled back, and looked into Maddy's eyes. Her head was level with mine. She was being lifted over the balcony. I've replayed it so many times. Everyone says she must have jumped, but she didn't. I saw it.

I still dream about her. Joy fills me as I see her face. But then I remember. In slow motion, her body silently bucks and writhes through the air. Her huge dark eyes hold mine, filled with fear and confusion. She falls away from me. My hands stretch out, but it's too late. She plummets to the ground and hits the concrete. Everything turns red.

I moved back in with Mum and Dad the next day.

Whenever I walk past the supermarket where the Heights used to be, I search for the spot of sky where I once lived. What happens to ghosts when buildings get demolished? Where is that ancient being now? I still think of myself as logical and down-to-earth, but these days my mind is more open than it used to be. The playing field where Joolz and I walked the dogs is still there. At the edge sits an old oak tree. On its trunk the words 'RIP Maddy' are carved deep into the centre of a heart.

ANGEL

Jo Gilmour

Daddy always wanted a boy.
Don't get me wrong, I never suffered none for it. I'm just tellin' you how it was. Daddy always wanted a boy.

But Daddy got me instead.

Okay, so… I was what you'd call a tomboy, and before you even think it, I'm not one of them lesbian girls that like to kiss other girls. Daddy calls them type of girls abominations to God and to Jesus. Just 'cause I act all boy-like don't mean I'm one of them – I'm just settin' you straight on that.

Now, any psychologist worth their money will tell you that I think all boy-like 'cause my daddy wanted a boy and given my "constant and fervent need to please him and make him happy" (their actual words) I was acting up like this, and that's why I am like I am. But I can tell you for now, that ain't the case. Not at all! Daddy told me I just don't think like women do. Daddy says women are weak and I believe him because my momma ran off when I was just a baby. Daddy don't like to talk about it, so we don't. Daddy said she just upped and left one day and that was that! I've seen hundreds of head doctors and people who want to open up my head and crawl inside. They all try, but I know how to play the game now. I'm pretty as a picture! No, really, I am. Butter wouldn't melt on my tongue. Big blue eyes, beautiful long blonde hair (Daddy liked it long.) I've got the look of the innocent, Daddy told me. I could tell them I've killed and they wouldn't believe me.

I'm only 12, by the way. You was thinkin' I was older, weren't you? I look older. I'm tall for my age and I like to bring justice to the perverts and fornicating sinners and abominations in the world. That's what Daddy said we do – we punish the unholy so they can go to heaven, as Jesus and God intended them too. Daddy told me it's our sacred mission, but we have to keep it secret 'cause it's our holy duty, but no man is safe, and **ALL** men can be lured from the righteous path of God. Now they've taken my daddy away.

It all started when I was 10 years old. I was walking through the scrub (a bit of wasteland that's owned by nobody, but it's a shortcut to our trailer) which Daddy had always told me to steer clear from, as all sorts of undesirables and crackheads live there. Well, I didn't believe him as I'd never seen any kind of house or dwelling there. But, like always, Daddy was right. One of them fuckers grabbed at me, and I was so lucky as I managed to duck. My bunches was just a second from getting snatched up. I span around and kicked that filthbag sinner real hard, straight in the balls, just like Daddy taught me. Y'all expecting me to tell you that I ran now, ain't ya? I did not run. I called my daddy.

Daddy was there within five minutes. He was **NOT** pleased, not pleased at all. I knew I was in trouble 'cause I'd been seen, and 'cause I'd made too much noise. Still, I frowned and stuck out my chin (my "fuck you" face as Daddy calls it, which makes him both proud and angry at the same time.) I regretted nothin'! But honestly, after everything Daddy had told me, it was far from flawless. The perv had ran off, but Daddy said that was okay, as there'd be others. Thinkin' about it now, it seemed like a bit of a test. I wouldn't put it past Daddy to teach me a lesson. Me disobeying him by walking through the scrub, at night, when he specifically told me not to. Y'all would expect me to get super mad at a stunt like that, but if it was a test, I can assure you it was for my own good. Daddy called me his little honey flower, on account of all the bees I helped him collect. I helped him catch lotsa bees. By bees he means sinners, and I'd tempt them, then Daddy would make me sit in the car whilst they were punished. Daddy told me that if anyone tried to hurt me or touch me in an ungodly way, they needed to be punished. Then we'd drive around and find a motel to stay the night. Daddy said **ANYONE**.

They took my daddy away.

I'd fallen asleep in the motel and Daddy had gone to get beers. My daddy had been corrupted by sinners, 'cause when I woke to him trying to take off my shirt, I knew he wasn't Daddy anymore. He called me honey flower and I brought my leg up to knee him in his "family jewels" and my, did he go into a rage! He was wheezin' and shoutin' and flailin' around like a lunatic. Daddy always told me that the devil came in many guises, and it was more than clear that I'd lost my daddy to the devil. He said Anyone. **ANYONE**. He said, "No man is inflammable when it comes to Satan and his ways," or something along them lines. He said it'd be hard and it'd be testin' at times, but I should always keep Jesus in my heart. So when he started pawing at me like a man possessed, I just knew that the badness needed to come out. When Daddy (devil) was laying on the floor wheezin', I shouted, "I'll save you, Daddy!" and scrambled off the bed for my daddy's bag, where he kept Angel (that's what he called his hunting knife.) He started shakin' his head and coughin', "No, No." But a demon would say that, right? I stomped on his chest and drew his head back in my hands, and the demon begged like Daddy said it would. But I was strong and drew Angel across his throat and watched the blood pour from his now grinning neck as I waited for the evil to flow from him and there was **A LOT**!

I waited.

I waited for my daddy to come back.

I waited for days.

I waited even when the flies came.

I waited while there was knockin' at the door, tappin' at first, then bangin', with voices shoutin' about calling the police.

I was just waiting for Daddy to wake up.

They kicked the door in and took my daddy away and took me to a special place, where they ask me lotsa questions. I told 'em what happened and they seem happy with that. I ain't told 'em everythin' though. I ain't told 'em that I've got a job to do.

I'm innocent.

Butter wouldn't melt.

I've promised and prayed to my daddy in heaven that I'll finish our work.

I'm goin' to a new home next week and I've hidden Angel in my bag. I'll make you so proud of me, Daddy…

MURDERABILIA

Adam Meyer

Louis was a collector at heart. That was how he ended up at the Colony Diner in East Meadow late on a Wednesday night, trying to decide between the cheeseburger and the lasagna. He still hadn't made up his mind when the guy in the frayed sportscoat slouched in. His hair was patchy like worn carpet and his nose hooked slightly to the right, like someone who'd boxed when he was young.

"You must be Louis," the man said, putting his hand out. "Ted Horwitz."

"You're late, Mr. Horwitz."

"For the record, it's Detective Horwitz. Nassau County Sheriff's Department." A cop? Louis hadn't expected this. But over the years he'd done business with eccentric millionaires and snot-nosed teenagers and little old ladies, so why not a cop?

"You said you had something I might be interested in." Louis knew he'd never be able to enjoy his meal unless he got this out of the way, whatever *this* was. The man's email hadn't been specific.

"All business, I like that." Detective Horwitz slid into the booth, his coat shifting to reveal the gun strapped under his left arm. The waitress started to come over, but Horwitz shook his head and she backed away.

"How'd you get my name, Detective Horwitz?"

"A friend of mine told me about you. He sold you some old comic books a while back."

Horwitz mentioned the guy's name. Louis couldn't picture him, but he remembered what he'd bought, some *Spiderman*s from the '60s.

"If you've got comic books to sell, save your breath," Louis said. "I've got plenty of those."

"Who said anything about comics?"

You did, Louis wanted to remind him, but held his tongue.

"My friend said you got some real cool shit, like a baseball signed by Babe Ruth. And some coin with two fronts on it."

"A 1907 double eagle."

"Must be worth a lot, eh?"

"For your information, Detective, I don't care about the money."

"C'mon, everyone cares about the money."

"If you're a true collector, an object's value has nothing to do with money."

Louis had understood this even as a kid, when he first started collecting. One Christmas his father gave him these superhero figures, dolls big enough to wrap your fist around, like Barbies. Even at seven he wanted the whole set, not just the popular ones like Batman and Superman but Aquaman and Captain America, too.

The waitress started over to the table again and this time Horwitz didn't stop her. He ordered the cheeseburger and Louis went with the lasagna. As she spun away, Horwitz said, "I heard you had something else, besides all that kid stuff."

Louis didn't like the way he said *kid stuff.* "Excuse me?"

"Heard you got a pair of hedge clippers. Used to belong to Joel Rifkin."

It was true. Six months ago, Louis had been in this very part of Long Island, prowling around yard sales, when this woman said she had a pair of hedge clippers that belonged to the notorious killer of nine women. "I borrowed them once and never got a chance to give them back to him. He lived right there, you know," she said, pointing across the street at a Colonial tucked behind a huge oak. While Louis couldn't be sure that Rifkin had ever so much as pruned a stray branch with those clippers, he did confirm that Rifkin had liked gardening and lived where the woman said, so why not? The hedge clippers only cost twenty dollars and he'd put them away and told himself that was that.

Now Louis started to sweat against the plastic seat, wondering where this was going. "I bought a serial killer's gardening tool. That's not illegal is it."

"Of course not. But if you're a collector and you like murderabilia, I thought maybe you'd be interested in something like this."

"Like what, Detective?"

By way of answering, Horwitz reached into his coat and for a moment Louis thought he was going for his badge. But Horwitz pulled out a cell phone, which he tapped and turned toward Louis. The screen showed a naked woman in a corner, her throat slit open, her skin a pale, washed-out color.

"That's Nora Forrester, a prostitute. We found her dead in her apartment about a year ago."

Louis nodded, feeling sick. He'd read about it in the papers. She was the third victim of the not-very-cleverly-named Long Island Slasher.

Horwitz tapped the phone again, calling up another photo. Louis shook his head. He'd seen enough.

"This one's not so bad, I promise."

Louis leaned in reluctantly. There was a picture of a white card with the number six – an evidence marker, like he'd seen on TV – and behind it a pair of underwear. Black, lacy around the edges, the kind of thing he'd only seen in Victoria's Secret catalogues.

"I could get them for you," Horwitz said. "If you're interested."

"Excuse me?"

"From the crime scene. The panties she was wearing the night she was killed."

"But that must be evidence."

"'Course it's evidence. Five crime scenes, we got lots of evidence, and we're still no closer to finding him. When we do – and we will – it won't be through forensics, and I don't care what you seen on CSI. We'll get him 'cause of a damn parking ticket, like the Son of Sam, or 'cause some neighbor saw him sneaking out in the middle of the night. And we'll need just enough DNA to match him to a couple of scenes and prove he's our guy."

Horwitz stopped talking when the food came. The lasagna was overcooked and dry. From the way Horwitz was going at his burger, Louis knew he'd made the wrong choice, though he didn't feel much like eating anyway.

"What you're talking about selling ... that's illegal."

"'Course it's illegal. But let me ask you something. You got yourself a nice house, don't you?"

Louis nodded. He had learned years ago to stop calling it his father's house, but he still thought of it that way, even though the old man was dead ten years already. Louis had stayed because he was comfortable there and because buying his own place and moving all the things he'd collected seemed like too much trouble.

"Me, I got *two* nice houses, one for my ex-wife and kids, the other for me and my girlfriend, and the county's strapped, cutting back on overtime. So, I need a little coin and I ask myself, what have I got that's worth anything? And who's it worth something to?"

Horwitz stared at Louis as if the answer were obvious. Louis pushed his plate away, supposing that it was.

"How do I know that what you're selling is real?" Louis asked.

"You got the picture to compare it to. And I'll bring the evidence receipt and the police report."

"But you could fake those, couldn't you?"

"I suppose. I guess you just gotta decide whether you trust me or not."

Louis nodded. Even the most shrewd collector could be duped. Louis knew an art expert in the Hamptons who owned a bunch of paintings by Picasso and Monet and never bought a new piece of art without the look-see of a dozen experts, and twice he'd acquired paintings that turned out to be fakes. "Do I feel like a fool?" he'd said. "Absolutely. But I took as much pleasure from those paintings as if they were real, and in the end isn't that all that matters?"

Louis saw the man's point. Sometimes you just had to decide whether or not you were buying what someone was selling.

"How much are we talking about here?" Louis asked.

Horwitz named a number. It was enough to take a nice vacation with, but Louis never went anywhere and he had plenty of money in the bank. But he wasn't going to overpay.

"Forget it."

"Hey man, you're not gonna find this on eBay or Craigslist, you hear me?" Horwitz said. "And if you don't want it, I got a long list of ghouls – I mean, guys – just like you, and they'll give me every penny I'm asking for, and maybe a few more."

Louis leaned back in the booth and realized something: he wanted this. He wanted it bad.

"Okay, it's a deal."

"A deal?" Horwitz grinned, signaling for the check. "In that case, dinner's on me."

* * *

Two weeks later, Horwitz brought the panties in a sealed brown paper bag with NASSAU COUNTY POLICE DEPARTMENT printed on the outside. Louis opened the bag just long enough to make sure he was getting what he'd paid for, but waited until the detective had left to take a closer look.

He ran his fingers over the cool silky fabric and inhaled. Nora Forrester's scent was still all over it. You're disgusting, he told himself, stashing the brown bag under his bed and thinking of her body slumped in a corner. He never should've bought the panties. But a week or so later he took them out of the bag again. The smell was still there, but his memory of the crime scene photo had faded.

Two months later, when Horwitz called and said he had something else to sell, Louis told him to come on by.

"You ever have one of those goddamn days?" Horwitz asked, already pacing as he came inside.

To Louis most days were the same, neither good or bad, but he nodded. He noticed that Horwitz wore a new sportscoat, one that didn't look like it had come off the rack.

"There's a new chief looking to make a name for himself, busy stirring up a lot of shit. Asking me all kinds of questions."

Louis felt an icy coldness in his chest. "About what?"

"Nothing that affects our business, don't worry. Anyway, take a look at this. It's from the last victim." Horwitz handed over his phone, which showed another crime scene photo. "You see that perfume bottle there on the dresser – well, she had two of them. The other one broke when she fought with the killer, whole goddamn room reeked of it. You can't even imagine."

But Louis could imagine, and did: the super-sweet scent of perfume in a room that already stunk of death, the woman's body in the middle of a rug scattered with broken glass. He closed his eyes and inhaled, detecting a faint whiff of vanilla.

"I brought the bottle in the picture, in case you're interested."

Horwitz held out a paper evidence bag. Louis reached in to touch the smooth glass of the bottle, searching for the places where the woman's own fingers might've lingered. The victim, Janice Pickard, had grown up in New Paltz and said she always wanted to be a big-time clothing designer. In her twenty-three years all she'd done was drop out of high school and sell her body for money.

"What do you think?" Horwitz asked, walking across the room.

Louis watched him go past a mountain of banker's boxes and stopped at the shelf where Louis kept a handful of his treasures on display. Horwitz picked up a baseball encased in Lucite, which had been signed by Mickey Mantle during the '63 World Series. Louis was an avid Yankees fan and his father had been one, too. Louis had bought the ball as a Father's Day gift when his old man was dying of cancer, but as soon as his dad saw it he said it was a goddamn waste of money and didn't want it. To save face Louis said that he sold it back to the dealer, but that was a lie. He'd stashed it in his underwear drawer until the day after the old man's funeral, and then he put it right there on the shelf.

"How much's this worth?" Horwitz asked, turning the object over in his hands.

"Five hundred, maybe." More like five thousand, but Louis didn't want the cop to know that.

"Fucking ridiculous. I mean, it's just a baseball, right?"

"It's not just a baseball. That's a memory, a moment in time. You can't put a price on that."

"Seems to me you can put a price on anything." Horwitz nodded at the perfume bottle in Louis's hands. "Speaking of which …"

∗ ∗ ∗

Louis had been keeping the panties by themselves, tucked away in a dresser drawer, but now he had the perfume too. One item was just something you owned, but two was the start of a collection, and any good collection needed a home. He brought out one of the sturdy wooden boxes that his father had trash-picked years ago. They were meant for collecting butterflies, but Louis had always been grossed out by the idea of a box full of dead insects.

Most of the time his new prizes sat untouched in their wooden box. For the next month or so he took them out maybe once or twice a week and then more often. He liked to hold the underwear, wrap his hands around it, and sometimes he'd spray a bit of the perfume on his fingers, not a lot, since the bottle was almost half-empty. Then he would touch the panties and smell the perfume and think about Nora Forrester or Janice Pickard. A couple times he even pulled out the Joel Rifkin hedge clippers from the closet and set those beside him, too.

Louis had no idea if Horwitz would call again, but he wasn't surprised when he did. What surprised him was the way Horwitz was acting, all preoccupied and jittery. "We got another Slasher murder," Horwitz said, his face drawn and haggard. "Number six."

"I haven't seen it on the news."

"Hasn't hit the news yet." Horwitz flopped down on the couch, looked around at the mountains of boxes, and shook his head. "All this shit, you must have some whiskey around. Get me a drink, all right?"

Louis found an unopened bottle of whiskey in one of the upper cabinets in the kitchen. It must've been there since his father died. Did whiskey go bad? He figured Horwitz would tell him if it had.

"The way he did this girl was different," Horwitz said, taking a long sip of whiskey. He didn't seem to mind the taste. "He kidnapped her from her own house but did his dirty work out on the beach, out by Glen Cove, right in the open. And man, it was ugly. He didn't just cut her throat, he hacked her up. Makes me think he's not getting the same old jollies he used to so he's trying some new things."

"If everything's so different, how can you be sure it's the Slasher?"

Horwitz looked at Louis and then away. "There's one thing we haven't put in the papers, something only he would know. This guy ..." He shook his head, like it was too awful to repeat. "... he cuts off their right pinky fingers and keeps 'em."

Horwitz reached inside his coat then, setting down a brown paper bag with some writing on the outside on the coffee table, said, "Anyway, I brought you something. I shouldn't do this, I know. But ... it's not like it's going to make any difference to her."

Louis's hand trembled as he reached across the table. His heart was pounding. He opened the brown paper bag cautiously and pulled out the gold chain, wrapped it around his fingers, studied the tiny diamond in the middle.

"It's hers?"

Horwitz nodded. "Lying right near the body. It's not worth shit, maybe a couple hundred bucks. But I know you're not worried about the resale value."

Louis spread the necklace across his palm, studying the diamond like a jeweler. The gold chain felt warm, as if from the victim's body heat. He wished he could go to the place where she'd been killed and touch her face, just once, ever so gently. Would Horwitz let him do that, for a price?

No, of course not. That was disgusting; why would he even think such a thing? He slid the necklace back into the paper bag, pushed it away from him.

"This isn't yours to sell."

"It's not anyone's, Louis. It's hers and she's dead."

"But her family—"

"Lives in Minnesota, hasn't talked to her in five years. And like I said, it's barely worth anything."

"But the memories…"

"Believe me, they got plenty of memories." Horwitz pushed the paper bag back to Louis. "More than they want."

* * *

Sure enough, about three hours after Horwitz left, the news about the Long Island Slasher's latest victim broke. Her name was Annabeth Benson. Louis found Annabeth's picture online and was disappointed to see she wasn't wearing the necklace. She hadn't been a prostitute like the other victims. She was a student at Nassau Community College, who worked part-time at a TGI Friday's in Garden City.

Over the next few days, he devoured every article that he could find about her murder. He found himself taking out the wooden box more and more often, sometimes five or six times a day. He also began to check the answering machine constantly, eager for another message from Horwitz. Sometimes he sat in front of the TV, running the gold chain around his fingers, wondering what it must have felt like to tear it from Annabeth's slender neck. He knew it was wrong to think about that. He had to stop. But he couldn't.

The next morning, Louis picked up the phone and put in Horwitz's number but he didn't press SEND, even though he had his speech all worked out: Nice doing business with you, but I've had enough.

Finally he decided that he needed to clear his head, so he drove out to Gary's Big Ink in Mineola. Gary owned the comic book store he'd named for himself and worked it alone most of the time, too. He was built like a wrestler, short and wide, with muscles that bulged whenever he brought a box out of the storeroom.

Louis was browsing the new releases when Gary plopped a crate of new graphic novels beside him and started talking. At first Louis was mostly tuning him out, until he picked up the words: "… terrible thing, and I'm not just saying that 'cause she was a customer."

"Excuse me?"

"That girl who just got killed, she used to shop here sometimes. Not many girls do, but she was a big fan of *The Walking Dead* and *Eternity Girl* and used to keep up with a few other books too. She lived right in the neighborhood, you know."

Louis hurried out of there, cruising down the back streets. He knew the address of the Slasher's most recent victim by heart and remembered that she lived in Mineola, but he hadn't thought about that when he drove out here. Or had he? It took some driving around, but he soon found the house where Annabeth had lived and been abducted from. It was a 1960s-era split level, completely unremarkable. The siding was scraped, the lawn ragged, the shades all drawn, but otherwise it didn't look any different from its neighbors. He wasn't sure what he'd been expecting. Police tape zigzagging every which way, maybe a cruiser to guard the place.

He got out of the car and crossed the sidewalk. The killer had stood here, perhaps on this very spot. What thoughts had gone through his head? Was he scared or excited or torn up over what he was going to do? Or did his brain just shift into autopilot, and let his body do the work? Louis reached into his pocket, half-expecting to find Annabeth's necklace there. He wished he'd brought it, fingers freshly doused with some of that perfume.

A neighbor boy, ten or eleven, scooted up on his bike, swerving to get around Louis, and looked at him warily. Louis turned away, and hurried back to his car.

On the way home he stopped at another comic book store – in the Roosevelt Field mall, where the bored clerk didn't know him – and bought recent copies of all the books that Gary said Annabeth had been a fan of. Then he made a detour to the beach in Glen Cove. It was deserted, the choppy surf gnawing at the sand. He walked up and down the beach, searching for the exact spot where Annabeth's body had been found, her right pinky clipped off. But as at the house, there was nothing to mark her life or her death.

* * *

That night Louis read the new comics he'd bought from cover to cover, Annabeth's necklace spread across his lap, and wondered what had appealed to her about these characters, these stories. At one point, he finally looked up and realized it was already four in the morning. What was he doing? Collecting was one thing, but he had crossed the line. He put the necklace back in the wooden box and then set the box in the closet with the other murderabilia. He would call Horwitz and tell him to take these things back, all of them. He didn't care about getting his money back, he just wanted this stuff out of his life.

But that wasn't meant to be.

The next morning he saw an article on the cover of *Newsday* about some detectives being arrested. Not for stealing evidence, but for taking bribes from a contractor. Louis recognized the face in the grainy photo, so he wasn't surprised to read Horwitz's name in the story. Apparently, Detective Horwitz was the ringleader of the illegal enterprise.

When Louis called Horwitz's cell phone, it went straight to voicemail. He left a message, and then another the next day, but neither was returned. The day after that the line was disconnected. Louis waited, but no one came knocking on his door. He didn't go out much, just sat around watching TV and eating junk food, and occasionally taking out his wooden box. But he didn't get the pleasure from it that he once had.

After a month, Louis began to think that maybe the police weren't going to come after all. Maybe Horwitz had been careful and no one had traced what he'd been doing.

And then the doorbell rang.

Louis felt a tightening in his throat. This was the

moment he'd been waiting for. He felt upset and anxious and defiant. Was it the cops? Could they just take his collection? Wouldn't they at least need to bring a search warrant? But hell, maybe it was worse than that. What if he went to jail for this? He and Horwitz in side-by-side cells? No, he wasn't going to do that, he couldn't stand it.

He looked out the window, expecting to see a row of police cars, but there was only a BMW convertible and a woman on the front step. He opened the door. The woman was tall and skinny and pretty, though she wore too much makeup and her tight jeans and low-cut blouse seemed better suited to someone just out of high school than in her thirties. Louis looked at her blankly.

"My name's Bridget," she said. "I'm a friend of Teddy's. I mean, Detective Horwitz's. Can I come in?"

She sat in the chair Louis usually sat in, but he didn't ask her to move.

"I guess you heard about what happened to Teddy?" she asked.

He nodded.

"Only a matter of time. I told him he was getting too careless, but he wouldn't listen. Turns out IA – Internal Affairs, that is – was all over him. He's working on a plea bargain, but there's a lot of evidence. It's going to be tough. He could be in jail for a damn long time."

"Did you know what Horwitz was doing?"

"Sure, I knew. I mean, not exactly but … who do you think bought me that convertible? Cops can't buy cars like that on a regular salary. I knew he had, ah, extracurricular activities."

"And did you know … what he was selling me?"

"That's why I'm here. Have you still got all that stuff?"

He found the wooden box in the closet and brought it over, feeling sheepish. He peeled back the lid so that she could see the collection inside, items placed on a silk cloth as if on display in a museum: the panties, the perfume, the necklace.

She didn't meet his eyes at first, and when she did she looked like she felt sorry for him.

"What?" he asked. "What is it?"

"Those things you bought from Teddy, they weren't … what you think."

"I don't understand."

"He bought those panties, ones just like the dead girl owned, and he … he made me wear them before he sold them to you. The perfume, he just picked up a bottle down at the mall."

"But the necklace—"

"That's just something an ex-boyfriend gave me. Teddy was only too glad to get rid of it."

He looked down at the things he'd collected and treasured so deeply, even though they were really worth nothing more than some second-rate artist's forgery.

"I'm sorry," she said.

"You should take these," he said, holding the box out to her. "They're yours."

She shook her head, ever so slightly. "No, they're yours. You bought them."

Yes, she was right. He had paid for them and they were his. He wondered if he could still get some pleasure from them, even if they weren't what he'd thought they were.

"In the beginning, of course, I wondered if they were real," he said, surprised to hear the words coming out of his mouth. "I guess I just wanted to believe, and somehow … maybe that was enough."

She nodded sympathetically and stood. "Look, I should go."

"No, wait." He was surprised at the high pitch his voice had hit. "I mean, not yet. Let me get you something to drink."

"You got a beer?"

He went into the kitchen, found a beer in the fridge, and hesitated. He looked back through the doorway at Bridget and thought of her underwear, her perfume, her necklace. He thought of all the times his father had sat in that same chair and made fun of his collecting, even though selling a few choice items had helped pay off the mortgage and even paid for the new roof. He bristled with energy and anger and desperation. He still needed the things in that box, and more than that he needed for them to be real.

"Does he know you're here?" Louis asked, handing her the beer with one hand, the other behind his back, hidden. "Detective Horwitz, I mean."

She shook her head. "Oh no, if he knew I was here, he'd be totally pissed. I didn't tell anyone I was coming. I just …" She tilted her head sideways, those huge eyes taking him in. "… I just thought you should know."

"Thank you for telling me," he said, turning, the kitchen knife balanced perfectly in his right hand as he reached for her. She started to scream but it was too late, the blade already at her throat. She bled a lot more than he would've guessed. He watched it come out of her, the blood, every last drop. He plunged the knife deeper in her chest than he could in her throat, feeling a satisfaction and a sense of power he had dreamed of but never experienced before.

When he was finished he looked down at the body, shocked. What had he done? Panic rushed through him. The things Horwitz had given him were frauds, so technically he hadn't done anything wrong. Until now …

What was he going to do? But he knew, of course. Dump her on the beach, just like the Slasher had done. Everything wouldn't be quite the same as in the other murders, of course. But he knew enough to make it convincing, and the rest didn't really matter. Horwitz himself had said that the Slasher had been mixing things up, changing his pattern.

Louis ran through the plan in his mind. He knew he would have to get rid of Bridget's car before any of his neighbors noticed. Then the body. But first, there was something else he had to do.

He found the old hedge clippers in the closet. He worked on her hand for a long time and it was bloody, gruesome work. He thought of stopping because it seemed so awful, treating a beautiful woman this way. But if he was going to make this seem like the work of the Long Island Slasher, then he had to follow the model.

When he was done he put her right pinky finger in the wooden box, beside his other treasures. After all, Louis was a collector at heart.

THE FIRST CIRCLE

Sue Eaton

'Look at this, Meg. What do you think it is?' My husband was holding out something that looked like a walnut. As I got closer, I realised it was a walnut, but it had been carved with an immense number of repulsive little faces.

'Here,' he said, trying to pass me the horrid little thing. 'The craftsmanship is brilliant.'

'No thank you. It's hideous.'

'I rather like it. It's different.'

'You can say that again. It looks like souls in torment. Put it back.' I could imagine the beady little eyes following me around, waiting for me to commit some sin so they could write it in my Book of Faults, all ready for Judgement Day.

He looked hurt, as if I'd criticised him personally. 'I thought you might buy it for my birthday.'

I did have to think about that. Men are notoriously difficult to buy presents for if they haven't a hobby. Aside from a pallet of bricks or a bag of cement, I was at a loss as to what to buy my husband for his approaching birthday, so I hesitated, which was a mistake. He took it as an affirmation.

'Where would you put it?' I asked, none too nicely.

'I don't know. Where do you think?'

'Anywhere I can't see it,' I suggested.

'Spoilsport. What's wrong with it?'

'It reminds me of scenes from Hell by that artist – what's his name? Doré?'

'So? I thought you liked Doré?'

I shrugged. In truth, Doré fascinated me, but I wouldn't give him wall space.

It seemed quite expensive for such a tiny thing, but then it was supposed to be carved with one thousand faces according to the lady who sold it to us. That was certainly a feat in itself and worth a bob or two. We managed to knock her down a bit because she couldn't produce any provenance, and once it was paid for my husband hid the tissue-wrapped devil nut in his jacket pocket before suggesting lunch. I guessed I wouldn't need to go to the trouble of wrapping the thing up as a birthday present.

On arriving home, hubby immediately looked for somewhere to display his new treasure. 'Why don't you put it on one of the plaque rails?' I suggested. 'There's space on the one over the arch between the sitting room and the conservatory.'

'Good idea. You being too short to see that high up,' quipped my dearest who was tall enough to just reach up and put the evil kernel in place without the use of a step. There it sat darkly, glaring malevolence over all it surveyed.

'Very nice, dear,' I said. But I didn't mean it.

I was up first, as usual, the following morning and came downstairs to find the horrid thing on the floor under the arch. Personally, I couldn't care less what happened to it, but my husband liked it and it did cost quite a bit, so I didn't think it would do to tread on it. I picked it up to put it somewhere safe. As it rolled from my fingers into the palm of my hand, I felt a sharp sting that made me go cold all over. Instinctively, I dropped the object that had apparently stung me, and I squeezed my hand tightly against the pain.

'What's up?' My husband had followed me down.

'Your kernel from hell had fallen from the plaque rail, but when I picked it up one of the faces bit me.' The pain was burning across my hand and up to my wrist. I felt my eyes start to water.

'Really? Is there any tea?' That was the sum of his concern over my plight.

'No. I was trying to put that... that thing safe.'

He picked up the nut from the floor and inspected it carefully before putting it back in its place. Apparently, it had survived me dropping it. He carried on through to the kitchen and I heard him rattling about with tea bags and mugs. The pain was lessening now, and I risked opening my hand and having a look. The fleshy part under my thumb, the Mount of Venus, was red and there was a tiny pinprick in the centre of the inflamed area. But by the time my husband came in with the tea, the redness had already receded and there was nothing really to show him. I felt a bit miffed and told him so.

That night I dreamed. I was in a dim, seemingly circular tunnel and the curved walls were covered with faces – little faces with moving mouths as if they were trying to tell me something, but I couldn't hear. I moved closer to listen and felt a sharp pain on the lobe of my ear. The pain woke me, and I could still feel a stinging around the lobe, as if I'd had a new piercing. I got up and inspected it in the bathroom mirror, but there was nothing untoward there aside from a little redness that I put down to sleeping awkwardly. I had difficulty in going back to sleep. Although the dream wasn't what I'd call a nightmare, I didn't want to go back into the tunnel.

The next morning the nut was again on the floor underneath the arch. I moved it out of harm's way with my toe, only to feel the same deep sting that made me go cold all over. I invariably go barefoot as we have underfloor heating. The pain was so intense I thought I would faint. I sat heavily on the nearest dining chair. When I looked down, I saw that the nut was attached to my big toe. I kicked at it with my other foot and managed to dislodge it. There was no way I was going to pick it up, besides I was feeling very weak and light-headed. I could swear the topmost faces were laughing at me. The feeling of fatigue lasted all day, and every time I sat down, I felt myself drifting towards sleep.

When I did fall asleep, I was back in the tunnel. The faces were laughing. I still couldn't hear everything they said, but the odd word fluttered across my consciousness like breath on a cool morning. I couldn't remember what was said when I awoke, but felt it was something unpleasant.

I went to bed as usual the next night, but as soon as I slept, I found myself wandering the curve of the tunnel listening and watching. There was the whispering again, becoming clearer and more and more hypnotic as the minutes passed. I still didn't understand the words, but somehow I knew that the horrid little faces wanted me to join them. The thought frightened me enough to waken me, and I got up sometime past midnight and spent the rest of the night downstairs, sitting in a chair trying to stay awake rather than risk returning to that chilling passageway.

The same happened the next night and the next and after a few days it reached a point when I made excuses not to go to bed.

Despite the feeling of abhorrence I had for the little nut, I was also fascinated by it and found myself touching it, aching for the sharp pain that preceded the feeling of lethargy.

'Why don't you see the doctor?' my husband eventually suggested. 'It's doing you no good this sitting up all night. He might give you something to help you sleep.' I found I couldn't tell him what was really happening. He wouldn't believe it.

'She,' I corrected him automatically. 'I'll be fine.' I didn't want to sleep.

But sleep I did, of course. I became so tired that I nodded off in the chair, and when I did, I found myself in the tunnel. I found I had missed the voices. I needed to know what they were saying and moved closer. I placed my left hand gently against the wall and felt it slide into the sea of faces. I pulled out in horror and woke cold and shivering in the chair. I held up the hand. It looked different – stretched and pale. I tucked it into my dressing gown. I needed help with this, but I was too tired. I would phone for an appointment when I felt better.

I tried not to look at my hand, but sometimes, of course, I needed to use both hands and saw them both together. I was right. It didn't look quite the same as the other.

That night I slept again. I put out my hand and felt it sucked into the sea of faces. This time I allowed it to take my arm as well, but woke to find my husband shaking me.

'You were shouting out.' He looked concerned. 'Were you having a bad dream?'

I risked a look at my arm and then hastily hid it away. 'I must have been,' I mumbled.

'You look very pale. Phone the doc, for heaven's sake.' I nodded.

I told myself I forgot to phone for an appointment. What would I say, anyway? How do you explain an arm so pale it looks almost transparent?

That night I was too enervated to stop myself being drawn into the wall of the tunnel. I felt my hand, then my arm, then my shoulder being drawn in, but the thought of my head joining the others frightened me enough to wake me up. I was too exhausted to move, and there was no sense of any feeling in my left side.

My husband was worried enough to phone the doctor and the doctor was concerned enough to send me to the hospital. I was too tired to be concerned or worried and just let them do as they pleased. I did rather hope I would be admitted and then perhaps the dreams would stop. They didn't. If anything, they became more intense, the faces more insistent, and I was too exhausted to resist them anymore.

I was sleeping more and more, wandering the unending channel, endlessly listening to their incessant murmurings. I slithered in and out between the faces, relishing the cool softness and the energy they gave. Until…

I could hear the nurse calling me from some distance and looked out from between the hungry little mouths. There was some sort of crisis happening around my bed and I watched with disinterest from my vantage point in the wall. Let them deal with it. I turned away from the ward and into the embrace of the hungry little faces.

THE BARBER

A.P. Sessler

Hey, new guy! You came back. That must mean you're serious about this, after all. For a minute I didn't think you had it in you, but I'm glad you proved me wrong. This is our latest customer here in chair Number One.

No, don't worry, sir. He's just going to observe for now. I'll be taking care of you today.

So yesterday we went over sharpening your razor. Today we're going over how to get a good lather.

We turn on the hot water. Let it run about 10 seconds to get good and piping hot. See that steam already? Our hot water heater's cranked to the max.

Next we get our brush. Wet it in the sink. Fully saturate the bristles. Then briskly rub the soap in clockwise circles with your brush a good 25 to 30 seconds. Some guys like to sing a little song. Whatever floats your boat and lathers your soap, I always say.

What am I using? Here at Bert's, we only use Dr. Lyle's Dream Cream. Just like the label says, It Cuts Like a Dream. You can read the ingredients if you like, but to sum it up it's formulated with an all-natural anesthetic tincture.

What's that, sir? Oh, don't worry. It's completely safe and regulated by the FDA. In fact, I couldn't even own this stuff if I didn't have a barber's license. Just sit back and relax, and you'll feel like a million bucks, trust me. There you go. That's good.

So yes, once you get a good lather up, apply liberally with your brush, making sure to fill in all those nooks and crannies. Pay special attention to the jawline, especially right where the ear meets the jaw. There we go. Cover everything up nice.

Beg pardon, sir? Oh, you're starting to feel it. Yes, it's nice isn't it? Thought you'd like that. Now just relax. I can't give you a proper shave if you keep talking. No worries, it's a common mistake.

Now we return our brush to the mug and get your razor. Since we covered sharpening yesterday, we won't go over that again but remember to make a few passes on your strop to remove any burrs on the blade. Yep, just like that. It's a good habit that will insure you don't scrape your customer's face to pieces.

What's that, sir? I can't understand a thing you're saying. Nope, not a word. You're just mumbling now. Shh.

Dr. Lyle's working his wonders. Your customer should always be relaxed like our fellow here. This is essential for a good shave. See? He's out like a light.

And now we begin. We take our freshly-stropped razor, draw the blade downward along the edge of the right ear like so, following the curve of said point where ear and jaw meet. You'll notice on some men, like our fellow here, that they don't have much of a jawline to speak of. No worries, we can be a little creative.

You might have to apply a bit more pressure to these trouble areas, but don't stop. Keep moving along the jaw, from your left to right. Now, a common mistake would be to continue on up the left side of the face, but this would involve quite the gymnastics.

Now we stop, remove the razor and place it along the edge of the left ear, repeat the downward motion and when you reach the bottom of the jaw, go from their left to right so that the present stroke meets the previous stroke. Make sure your ends connect.

Now that we've made the initial stroke, the top will be much easier, as it can be executed without worry of injury. Start at the edge of the right ear, the same point we did before, but this time draw the razor upward, following the hairline if there is one. Otherwise, you can continue the stroke until you meet the edge of the left ear.

Use a slight clockwise twist of the wrist whenever you come to a curve. Almost there. And there we have it, a nice smooth stroke.

Oh my, almost forgot. You mind shutting the barber pole off? It's the plug right there. Runs under the mat and beneath the door, so just follow the extension cord until you come to the fork in the road, so to speak. Yep, that's it right there. Pull that out. And be sure to lock the door. We like to give each customer our undivided attention.

Alright, back to business. Come close. Closer. Don't be shy. You'll want to see this part as it's pretty important.

Make sure the edge of the blade moves in a smooth, steady motion, left to right, parallel to the right brow. When you reach the far end of the left brow, twist the wrist clockwise, but not too much, 15 degrees or so will do, then circle the eye and reverse the direction of the stroke right to left.

Follow the bridge of the nose with a slight slope as if you were drawing a pair of glasses, or as I like to think of it, the "bandit's" mask a raccoon wears – whatever makes your work more enjoyable, I always say!

When you reach the far end of the right eye complete the stroke with another clockwise twist of the wrist. Remember, not too much or you may injure yourself.

Once the stroke is complete, perform a similar cut around the mouth, again starting with their right, moving to their left. Be sure to give yourself about an inch margin around the lips or the final stroke will not be clean.

Alright, that's it. Go ahead and rinse your razor. We're done with it for the time being. Now for the final step.

We grab the bottom flap of skin – what I call the collar. Don't be afraid to get your fingers in there – you won't hurt anything. Now pull upward, firmly, steadily, mindful not to go too fast or you may tear something. If you need to, stop, take a breath, give yourself – and your hands – a rest. Remember: slow and steady wins the race, I always say.

Continue pulling upward, paying special attention to the mouth and eye area. If your strokes are well defined you shouldn't have any trouble, but these are the areas where any shortcomings will definitely bite you in the butt. Keep on pulling until you reach the crown and you will hear the satisfying sound of a well-skinned head.

Ah, you noticed. Dr. Lyle's is also a blood coagulant. Keeps us from making a mess or having to clean one up. I told you, it cuts like a dream.

Go ahead and give the skin a good rinse and leave it in

the sink until we're ready. Make sure you have the stopper in and fill it about a quarter full of ice-cold water. The colder the better. Remember: hot for cutting, cold for curing.

For the finishing touch we take a nice, clean towel and lay it upon the customer's face. This really opens up the pores, gives the face some room to breathe. That's a little trade humor. Lighten up, kid.

Oh. Someone's at the door. Don't worry about the barber pole. Leave it unplugged. Now hurry, let him in before he walks off.

Welcome stranger, come on in! Have a seat right there in good ol' Number Two. My assistant will be with you in just a moment, so make yourself comfortable.

Can we do a what? Oh no, son, I'm sorry. We don't do those fancy dos here. We're a one-size-fits-all barbershop. We do one cut and we do it well. But don't you worry your pretty little head, we'll have you done in a jiff, just ask our last customer ... well, he might not be much of a talker, but his smile says it all.

Oh, right. He's having his facial at the moment, so you'll just have to take my word about that smile. And trust me, by the time we're done you'll be wearing one just like it.

LUNA TOO

Jess Doyle

Yellow roses rambled across the cottage's craggy stonework. A clematis clung to it. Pale blue flowers like pastel stars fading in the afternoon light.

'It's tiny,' Luna's dad complained as they sat in the car, gazing out at the little house that would be their home for the week.

'We'll be out every day anyway,' Luna's mum said. 'Besides, it's so pretty. That must be Brian.'

Luna looked past the flowers to a tall, thin man who stood by the front door waving a set of keys. She squinted as the sun bounced off his bald head. He had dark shadows around his eyes, as though time had beaten him up. Luna didn't like the look of him. When she got out of the car, she discovered that he smelt of stale cigarettes and his clothes were dirty.

It took the caretaker, Brian, all of a minute to show them around. The little cottage had once been a one up, one down. Downstairs had a modern extension to house a small kitchen and an even smaller bathroom. The stone stairs were narrow and very steep. Luna's mum was concerned by them and made it very clear to Luna that she wasn't to use them on her own. There was just one bedroom, so Luna would sleep on a pull-out bed.

The garden was enchanting. At the back of the house

the colours were soft pinks, white and blues. There were copious roses, lavender bushes swarmed with pollen-drunk bees, cosmos floated on clouds of frothy foliage, and spears of hollyhocks and larkspur reached for the sun. The patio had a wooden picnic bench bordered by lanterns and fairy lights. Luna's dad said they'd have barbecues all week. He was busy unpacking the car while Luna's mum chatted to Brian.

'It's called Ty Dewin. It means "Warlock House",' he said.

Luna hadn't been listening until then. 'Warlock, like a man witch?' she asked.

'Yep, a real-life warlock built this place,' he told her. 'It's very old.'

Luna's mum put a hand on her shoulder, mistaking her interest for fear. 'Of course, it's just a name. Brian isn't saying that there were really warlocks,' she reassured her daughter.

Luna glared at her mum. 'There *are* real warlocks,' she said.

'I'm a descendant of the warlock that built this place,' Brian said.

Luna looked at him with a new interest but detected nothing magical in him. 'Does that mean you're a warlock too?' she asked doubtfully.

'No, I'm a gardener,' he told her. 'Although, gardening is a type of magic.'

'No, it's not,' Luna said.

Luna's mum was about to say something about manners, but Brian laughed. 'If you're interested in magic, you'll like the older part of the house. There's a genuine witches' mark in the fireplace. I'll show you.'

He pointed out a mark that had been etched into the wood around the hearth. It was just a couple of interlocking triangles inside a circle.

'Do you know what a witches' mark was for?' Brian asked Luna.

She shook her head.

'Protection against evil spirits. Folk used to believe that demons could get in through the chimney,' he said, tapping the stone chimney breast with a dirty fingernail. 'The old warlock must have been pretty paranoid about it, 'cos we reckon he put a dry cat in the wall too. Bet you don't know what a dry cat is, do you?'

Luna shook her head.

'I don't know what a dry cat is either,' Luna's mum said.

'I'll tell you,' Brian said with a grin. 'In the olden days they used to think that cats were psychic. Do you know what that means?'

Luna looked unsure and then shook her head.

'They thought that cats could move between worlds, understand things we don't and see things that we can't,' he said.

'They can,' Luna said. 'Our neighbours got a cat and I see her all the time staring at things no one else can see.'

Brian chuckled and it infuriated Luna. 'It's true.'

'Well, you might be right,' he said.

Luna's mum had placed her hand back on Luna's shoulder and could feel her tense up. 'Luna loves cats,' she said. 'She'd love to have one but her dad's allergic.'

''fraid so.' Luna heard her dad's voice from the kitchen doorway.

'So, what's a dry cat then, Brian?' Luna's mum asked

intrigued, despite not being entirely happy with the conversation this man was having with her daughter.

'Well, 'cos they thought cats were psychic, they'd sometimes brick them into walls when they built a new place. That way the cat would be there forever to guard the place from evil.'

Luna was quiet while she thought about it. She looked around the room trying to decide where the cat in the wall might be. Her eyes fell on the fireplace.

Her dad stepped into the room. 'So, there's a dead cat in the walls?'

'Well we don't know for sure…'

'Was it already dead?' Luna interrupted. 'When they put it in the wall. It wasn't alive, was it?'

Her mum answered quickly. 'Oh, no, the cat would had died of old age first. It would have had a lovely long life.'

Brian chuckled again and this time Luna felt her mum's hand tense on her shoulder.

'Some guests reckon they've seen its ghost.'

Luna gasped excitedly. 'Really? A ghost cat? Have you seen it?'

'Not me, no. Plenty of others, though.'

'What colour cat is it?' Luna asked.

'Most have said white or grey, but one guest said they'd seen a cat the colour of moonlight,' Brian said.

Luna's eyes lit up; she turned to look at her mum. 'She's the moon, like I am. She's Luna too.'

'You be sure to look out for her,' Brian said.

'We will.' Luna noticed the irritated tone in her mum's voice. 'I think that's quite enough ghost stories. Thank you, Brian.'

'Well, if you need me for anything, I'm just the other side of the copse at the back there.' He gestured towards the back of the house.

'Thank you again,' Luna's mum said, ushering him out the door.

Luna's dad smiled at her once the door was shut. 'It's alright, she's not frightened. Are you, my little moonbeam?'

'I hope I get to see the ghost cat,' said Luna.

'See?' Luna's mum frowned. 'He should know better than to creep out a little girl.'

'I'm not creeped out, Mummy.'

'Come on Luna, time to explore the garden,' her dad said.

Amongst the flowers, Luna wondered if she'd been wrong when she'd said there was no magic in gardening. She searched the flowerbeds and ventured into the shady copse expecting to find fairies at play. She thought of her neighbour's cat with her wide amber eyes and she concentrated hard, trying to find a cat's focus and see the magic she sensed around her.

* * *

Luna didn't argue much at bedtime. She was excited about the first full day of the holiday and the thought of spending it at the beach. She was hoping to see a mermaid, but her dad said it wasn't likely because mermaids were very shy.

'Can we leave some milk out for Luna Too?'

'Luna Too?' her mum asked.

'The ghost cat,' Luna said.

'I don't think that's a good idea, love. We don't want to attract mice.'

'Please?'

Luna's mum acquiesced. 'I suppose a little in a saucer won't do much harm.'

Luna placed the dish beside the fireplace. She climbed the steep stone steps up to the bedroom and her mum tucked her into the pull-out bed. Once she was asleep, her parents sat out on the patio and shared a bottle of wine.

* * *

In the morning Luna's dad woke up to a fit of sneezes; his eyes were streaming.

'Trust you, first holiday for two years and you get a cold on day one,' Luna's mum said.

'It's Luna Too,' Luna said. 'Dad's allergic.'

Her parents laughed, which made Luna frown.

'I don't think you can be allergic to a ghost cat, love,' her mum said.

'Maybe I'm a little bit allergic to the house, though,' her dad sniffed. 'Old houses can be dusty and damp – maybe that's triggered it. A bit of sea air ought to clear it.'

Once they were downstairs, Luna went straight to the saucer by the fireplace. 'I think she had some. It looks like it's less to me. What do you think?'

Her mum looked doubtfully at the dish. 'Maybe. I don't know. Maybe ghost cats don't need to drink.'

'Maybe they don't but maybe they like getting little presents anyway, even if they can't do anything with them.'

* * *

Luna inhaled the salty air and stared at the horizon, but the sun reflecting on the sea hurt her eyes. Maybe she wouldn't see a mermaid, but it was a good day anyway. She paddled and splashed in the sea. She built a sandcastle fit for a sand-queen. She ate chocolate ice cream and she found beautiful seashells and searched for fossils. She was tired at the end of the day and the walk back to the car seemed to go on forever. She fell asleep on the drive back to the cottage, and when her parents woke her she could smell the fish and chips they'd picked up while she dozed. Her dad said he couldn't face setting up the barbecue again.

Luna sat in the armchair picking at fat, greasy chips; she hadn't eaten much of the fish. 'Cats like fish. Can I leave some of mine for Luna Too?'

'I don't think leaving food around is a good idea, love,' her mum replied. But Luna managed to slip a couple of flakes of soft, white fish from her plate onto the floor beside the fireplace. Her parents didn't notice.

Her dad had begun to sneeze again since they'd got back to the cottage, so they went to sit out on the patio. Her parents opened another bottle of wine and agreed that Luna could stay up late. She listened to her parents chatter as she stared dreamily at the night sky and her namesake beamed down at her. It was a clear night and Luna had never seen the sky so full of stars. Her mum pointed out a couple of constellations. Luna couldn't see the shapes that her mum could, but she loved looking at them anyway. Once she thought she'd spotted Brian through the trees, but her parents hadn't seen. When she could barely keep her eyes open, her dad, ignoring the protests, carried her up the steep stairs to her little pull-out bed.

* * *

Luna jolted awake. In her dream she'd heard a furious yowl. It had sounded like the noise her neighbour's cat made when it got into a night-time scrap with a local tom. She sat up in her bed and for a second it seemed the bedroom was flooded with soft silver light. Then it was dark. She heard a crash, loud enough that she felt it too. A moment later she could hear her parents' voices downstairs. There was something urgent in their tone, but hushed too. They didn't want to wake her. She lay back down and listened for a while, but tiredness got the better of her and she closed her eyes. Soon a gentle purring was lolling her back into a peaceful sleep. She felt something soft and warm nestle up beside her.

Downstairs, Luna's parents gawped at the blood pooling at the foot of the steep, stone stairs. At the still body and the skull that seemed almost flattened against the solid stone floor. They couldn't understand how Brian had managed to slip past them on the patio. Perhaps he'd used a key and come in through the front door. They puzzled as to how he'd fallen; perhaps he'd tripped on something on those steep stairs. They didn't dare think about why he had sneaked into the cottage while they were tipsy on the patio and their little girl was alone upstairs, but they exchanged looks that spoke of both horror and relief.

Upstairs, Luna slept soundly and dreamed of a cat the colour of moonlight.

ROXY

Viktoria Faust

Today is my last day with Roxy. Soon she goes to a new farm and it's hard to part with her. My mom always tells me not to give them names, because if you name something it's harder to say goodbye – you get sentimental. But I cannot help myself. Sometimes I just have to. With Roxy I had to. There's something in her. When she looks at me I feel it's almost as though she can understand me.

Of course, I know that she really does not understand. I'm not a little girl anymore. I'm thirteen now and I understand that Roxy is only an animal and that she cannot understand, but sometimes I like to think that she can and that in her brown eyes I can read something I like to interpret as reason. But no, indeed, Roxy is just an animal, and a very dangerous one if you allow it to be what it is.

Farms like ours are not rare. They have them all over the country and the State finances them. Of course, there are a number of those who oppose them. Because of this, each farm is guarded by a small army that is also funded from the State's budget, because in the past it has often happened that farms such as ours are attacked by activists of the Animal Protection Society. This, of course, happens less frequently now, especially after the security measures had been intensified, but there are still individuals who will do everything to force farms like ours to close.

Mom says they're fools. They do not even realize how good life is to them. Mom does not remember times before, but she remembers what her mom and her grandmother told her. Sometimes she tells me those stories, but I do not really like to listen to them because then I have nightmares.

While Roxy is prepared, with a dozen others ready for today's shipment, I sit and watch. They wash them, cut their hair, give them final vaccines. Now and then Roxy looks at me and every time I feel as if my heart skips a beat. Tomorrow, her pen will be cleaned and a younger animal will replace her. And Roxy will be no more. She'll live for another year or two, though. I do not know exactly what their life span is after they leave their breeding farms. Roxy is healthy and genetically suitable. This will allow her a few more years of life. And then, like all the others which reach maturity on the farm, her organs will be collected and stored.

I like to think that's the way Roxy will be able to continue to live. Of course, that's just one of my fantasies. They do not really live on. They're just animals. They have their purpose. Without it, none of them would live.

The animals don't make much noise. Their vocal cords are cut. Mom says that this practice is new, that the first farms did not have the custom of cutting the vocal cords and that the racket the animals made was horrible. Also, their front and back legs are broken so they can never walk properly. In the best cases they are lame and have difficulty moving quickly; in the worst cases they are completely paralyzed. But that's even better, Mom says. Let one of these beasts escape and I can imagine the panic that would cause. Our farm is near the city. I can imagine the headlines in the papers. But newspapers always exaggerate. No animal has ever hurt me and I've lived on the farm my whole life. Of course, sometimes babies can bite you if you let them, but I guess that's the case with all cubs.

Mom says that the animals' behavior is soothed by sedatives, and I cannot really imagine how these animals would look without its beneficial effect. Sedatives are in the water they drink and their food.

Otherwise, we run our own farm according to ecological principles. So, we are careful what we feed our animals with, and we take care of them so they live comfortably. If they were left to their own devices, they would not know how to take care of themselves; and that's why they live a good life – Mom's words again. Mom says that even in the past, when "in the wild", they were not able to take care of themselves. They always depended on us. That is why the State did well when it put them in farms and restricted their breeding, which no longer allows them to be "in the wild", because that way they are not able to harm either themselves or others. This is a better future. A safer future.

But sometimes I feel like we are doing something wrong. Not that my Mom is wrong or that the whole system is wrong, but I sometimes wonder (I have a habit of wondering): Why are the attacks of the Animal Protection Society so brutal? Why in their protests do they call us by insulting names and what exactly is a "sadistic beast" and what is "inhumane"? What are "animal rights" and why do people who eat meat and wear leather shoes and belts strive to legalize them? We at least do not skin our animals, and we do not walk in their skin. Our animals have a lifespan that they could otherwise only dream of and live a comfortable stress-free life because such are the rules on an eco-farm. And I wonder how many protesters have organs picked up on farms like ours, organs that have saved their lives, lives of their children, some of their family members? That's hypocrisy, Mom says. And I agree. How is the life of one animal different from the life of another? But no matter I agree, this does not mean I do not doubt. And wonder. And that's why I'm often thoughtful, because I cannot find the answers to most of my questions.

The last time the Society attacked one of the farms they killed everyone there. All those soldiers, all the workers, the whole family who ran the farm: a mother with four children. They took all the animals. I do not know where they took them. I suppose to one of the illegal farms, but I really do not know how that might be different or better. We take good care of our animals, make sure that they are short of nothing. How could an illegal farm be better for them? And how could that be more "humane"? So many lost lives. And why?

These are the things I'm wondering about and why I'm so thoughtful. And when I'm thoughtful I like to go to the pens and sit with Roxy. And that's why it's going to be hard for me when she's gone.

Roxy looks at me again and breaks my heart. All animals are shaved very short when they reach a certain age. Hairiness indicates their maturity to go to the other breeding farm. Approval for acceptance on a breeding farm is a sign of great genetic particularity and I am therefore proud of Roxy, probably as much as I'm sad she's going. But Mom says if Roxy hadn't been selected to go to the breeding farm she wouldn't have stayed with us for this long anyway. Animals which are bred only for organs do not last more than nine years. Roxy is thirteen, as I am.

Mom comes in. She sits beside me on the fence of the pen and we both are watching the herd's preparation. After a while Mom looks at me and asks: "Roxy?"

I just nod my head. And Mom nods her head, but in the opposite direction, disapprovingly, but without reproach. She knows I have a soft heart. Especially for Roxy. And maybe because she too has a soft heart, and especially towards Roxy, Mom says nothing more. Silently, we continue to watch the workers as they finish the preparations, and every time Roxy looks at us (and she does it a few times) my heart breaks. That's how you are supposed to feel when you lose someone you love, human or animal – it does not matter. The heart knows no difference.

"They are born for that, you know," Mom finally says. I know, but it does not lessen my sorrow. Everything is so sad in the end, all those goodbyes. Actually, it seems to me, after Roxy I will not love anyone anymore. Roxy was different. Roxy I loved more than even the cutest cub we ever had on the farm, though Roxy never was very cute, not even when she was young – judging by the pictures, because I do not remember that time because I was little at the time myself. I believe I know why it is so and I believe I know why my mom allowed me to spend all that time with her. Maybe Mom in her heart hides the same kind of sadness; she's just better in hiding it than me. But if that's the case, I wonder what mother's reasons were for leaving Roxy on the farm. Because it is not customary; in such cases, the animals are given to another farm, just because of the possible sentimental connection. Not all people are strong enough and not all fit to be farmers. But I suppose Mom is. Because if I'm right, for Mom this is also a horrible day. She just does not show it. She's a bit sad, but looks like she's sad because I'm sad. And though she's looking at a group of selected animals, Mom not once looks Roxy in the eye. When I think about it, I do not remember ever seeing her do that.

"Are you sad too?" I'm asking, just in case. Mom's face is pale. Her forehead wrinkles. This time she doesn't want to meet my eyes either.

"They're animals. Dangerous animals. They kill, rape and destroy. They cannot be allowed to go around without supervision, to do evil. This is the best thing we can do with their faulty lives. Their organs will save the lives of those who are not born with mutated chromosomes. Their seeds will help create new Citizens of the World. And that's how they become useful. It will help humanity. That's just Roxy, Maxxine. They are all r.o.XY. It stands for recycled organs with XY chromosome. It could have been your sister, but it will never be your—"

Mom uses a word I do not understand, which I have never heard and which I forget. All she said, all these words, are strange and somehow indignant, and I think Mom says them out loud more for herself than for me. I know nothing can change. But I wonder if my Mom is trying to convince herself and if she will ever be able to forgive herself.

I watch as they take away Roxy and the others. Roxy turns, looks at me for the last time with the same brown eyes as my own are, and Mom's too. Mom does not look back, but I watch all the way while Roxy is taken away from the barn, while I still can see her and she looks at me as well. I know I should say "he", but in the world we live in we do not have male gender and male names. That's why Roxy is only Roxy, with the wrong chromosome in her name, a mistake of nature, my not-to-be twin sister.

I know Mom is sad because she turns and goes away and I feel sorrow in the sound of her footsteps, but I will never feel it in her words. For a moment I look for Roxy and then I jump from the fence and go after Mom. I know she'll need me today.

A LITTLE DEATH

Ryan Harville

There are things that no one talks about when you lose someone. You really don't know until it happens to you, until it changes the fabric of your world. No one tells you how your voice falls flat in an empty room; the words float there as if waiting for a response, an echo, *anything*. Nothing comes but silence.

Looking back, with the burden of hindsight, it all happened so quickly. We were told that if my wife ever conceived, the chances of going to full term were slim. They said she may be in danger if she even *attempted* to carry a child to full term. We didn't listen. We were going to make life, something that was part of both of us. A beautifully crafted gift to the world.

I have no excuses. It was a dangerous combination of youth, naivety, and stupidity.

Kate carried our daughter, Diana, nearly six months. She went into early labor and lost a lot of blood. It was a blur of noise and motion. Nurses yelling, monitors beeping and screeching.

And above it all, Kate screaming. *"Save her! Please, save the baby!"*

They performed an emergency c-section, and my Diana was delivered.

She never drew a breath.

Not one.

The doctors were very kind. They let me hold Diana for a while. I kept her wrapped in a pink and blue blanket. I pushed a chair near Kate's bed and sat with them both, describing our dead daughter's features to my dead wife.

"She has your nose, Kate!" I said excitedly. "She has your nose, and my eyes, and they don't see, won't see don't see won't see…"

This continued, devolving into a sort of mania. I laughed and howled and sobbed, and when the nurses came for Diana I screamed.

Security eventually showed up and escorted me to another wing of the hospital and I was admitted for forty-eight hours of observation. For my own good, I was told, which was probably true. When the doctor suggested a sedative, I didn't argue. I wanted oblivion, wanted to forget. If a pill would do that even for a short while, I would take it happily. And I did.

A few days after being discharged from the hospital we had the funeral. It started off badly, and got worse. Her family insisted it be in a church and I didn't fight them on the issue. Neither Kate nor I were believers, but I knew she was beyond caring either way.

There were the normal things you'd expect. An old woman played the pipe organ. People told me how sorry they were. Then I got into an argument with her father. He said that God must've needed my wife and child in Heaven, that they had a greater purpose there.

I told him to shut his goddamn mouth.

The notes from the organ came to an abrupt stop and I could feel everyone's collective stare as my cheeks burned with the heat of rage. My mother-in-law tensed, and her mouth was shut so tightly that her lips turned into a thin, white line. But she didn't say anything. She took his arm and they walked away, both pale and quiet.

I wish I would've just nodded, pasted on a fake smile, and walked away. They had lost their daughter and granddaughter. I should've just let them find comfort however they wanted, but it infuriated me. What would God need with my wife? What could possibly be so fucking important that He needed a newborn? Idiocy, all of it. But it wasn't the best time to take a stand on it, I know that. They deserved to grieve as much as I did.

The real trouble started with Kate's brother, Matt. Alcohol and Matt were no strangers to one another, and they had apparently met earlier that day.

In the parking lot, after the funeral, Matt walked quickly toward me. I thought maybe he was coming to offer condolences, or just say hello, or something. I should've seen it in his eyes, but…I'd just buried my family, you know? My powers of perception weren't really that great at that moment. He barreled into me, shoving me against my car. My back struck the window, shattering it as the car alarm let out a nasally high-pitched whine.

"Why?" Matt yelled, his hot, whiskey-laden breath on my face. He smelled like he hadn't bathed in days, and his beard was wild and unkempt. "You ever heard of *adoption,* you selfish son of a bitch?!"

Maybe I was struggling to hear him over the blatting of the alarm, or maybe I just couldn't believe what he was saying. Matt had always been nice to me before. People were stopping, staring at the spectacle.

"What did you just say to me?" I cried. "What the *fuck* did you just say to me?"

He pushed me back again, his hands gripping the lapels of my coat. "You've could've adopted! Hell, you could've gotten a fucking *dog!* But no, you had to talk her into it. *This is your fault*—"

I hit him, cutting him off midsentence. I didn't even think about it, just pushed him back with one hand and swung the other. My fist connected with his jaw and he fell to the asphalt. I thought it was over, but I was wrong. I turned to get into the car, holding my throbbing hand to my chest, and then his hands were grabbing my head and slamming it against the doorframe.

It was my turn to hit the ground, and Matt jumped on me, punching me until I choked on blood. The world went dark around me, except for the scattered pieces of glass reflecting the weak sunlight. Soon that was gone too, and I slipped into unconsciousness.

I didn't press charges and neither did he, but it was the last time I saw any of her family. No one called or visited, which was fine. I didn't care. About them, or anything else.

The silence. A lack of sound, yes, but everything else was muted as well. Colors were paler, smells almost nonexistent.

So, you can imagine how I felt when I smelled my wife's perfume late one evening, three weeks after the funeral.

I came home from work, only my third day back, and as soon as I stepped across the threshold I could smell it. Sweet and floral, but subtle. It lingered in the air, as if she had just walked by recently, passing through on the way to our bedroom maybe. I let out a shaky sigh and shut the door with a trembling hand. The clatter as I dropped my keys on the nearby table was deafening in the quiet room.

I threw my coat over the back of the couch and headed straight for my bedroom. Evening naps had become routine. So much easier than facing reality. Usually I would get up, shower, then go back to bed. Some nights I'd eat dinner, but that had become rare. Some nights I didn't even make it to the bedroom, I'd just wake up sore and stiff on the couch the next morning.

The scent was stronger in the bedroom, strong enough for me to believe I was having another episode. A "momentary break from reality" the doctor called it while I was under observation. I laid across the bedspread and buried my face in a pillow, succumbing to the hot tears that had been threatening to spill all day.

I really let go, moaning and yelling, trying to drive out some of the pain through sheer volume.

"Scott?"

I jumped, and not figuratively. I was up and on my feet in seconds, wiping at my face.

Standing in the bedroom doorway was my wife. Kate looked tired but otherwise fine, still wearing the dress she had been buried in. It was pristine and moved around her ankles as if pushed by a subtle breeze.

You watch movies, read books, hear stories. But nothing can ever prepare you for a moment like that. All the world's fiction can't come close to explaining how it feels to see a miracle.

I hit my knees, softly sobbing. "Please be real," I said, my teeth clenched. "Please be real, please be real—"

She wrapped her arms around me and whispered. "Shhh. I'm here, and that's all that matters for now."

We held each other for a long time, my face pressed against her dress. Eventually we kissed, made our way to the bed, and made love in the dark.

I woke in the early hours of the morning to the sounds of birds chirping, like in a movie. Kate's face was brightened by the sunlight that filtered through the window blinds. Her skin was perfect. She had always had great skin, but this was different. There was a softness to it, an ethereal quality.

I then realized that it wasn't a trick of the early morning light. I really could see through her, though not completely. It was like looking through a veil of smoke.

She had woken up at some point and was looking back at me. I didn't bother to hide my surprise; I was too stunned to even try.

"Kate, what is this?" I whispered. "What is going on, how're you here—"

She shook her head slowly. "It doesn't matter, does it? I'm here."

"I can almost see through you."

"I know," she said. "But...but it will get better. *I* will get better. As long as you love me."

I ran my hand slowly over her shoulder and down her arm, relishing the texture. "You feel real. Are you real, Kate? Have I gone crazy?"

She smiled. God, I had missed her smile. "You're not crazy. I'm here. You can see me, hear me, touch me. I am real," she said, grabbing my hand in hers. She pulled me towards her and placed my hand between her legs. "This is real."

As I said earlier, fiction can't prepare you for witnessing the impossible. My wife had come back to me, a miracle, and there I was staring at my haggard face in the bathroom mirror.

I had the flu. Or at least it sure felt like it.

It seems laughable, really. We were a pair, the miracle and the mundane. I was shivering and shaking. It hadn't really gotten its hooks into me, but I could feel it gathering strength.

Almost two weeks had passed. I had quit my job, and we were living entirely off Kate's life insurance payout. See? The mundane sounds strange given the right circumstances. We spent our time talking and laughing, making love and sleeping. We never spoke of the in between, the time she was gone. I once broached the subject, and she just shook her head, her face stern, almost angry. I didn't ask again after that.

For the most part, we were happy.

Another week went by, and I was feeling worse. Awful, really. No congestion or anything, just feeling rundown and faint. I thought then it may have progressed to some sort of infection. It never really occurred to me to seek help. I was with Kate, and that was all I needed.

And she was faring much better. I couldn't see through her at all, even in bright light. She had gained a little weight, which was strange. She hadn't eaten a bite of food since her return.

She came to me that night, wearing nothing but a smile, her dark hair flowing like a cascade over her shoulders.

"I came to see how you're feeling," she said. Before I

165

could answer, her searching hand was beneath the sheet. "Hm. You feel pretty good to me."

My laugh turned into a cough. My raw throat felt like it was full of fishhooks. "Thanks, but I feel terrible, babe. Raincheck?"

Her smile faded. "You don't want me?"

I shook my head. "No, no, it's not that *at all*. I'm just really tired. Let me rest awhile and maybe—"

She looked down towards the sheet, her hand still moving. "*This* doesn't feel tired."

"I know, but—"

She threw the sheet back. "Just lay still."

"No, seriously—"

"Lay. *Still*," she said, her voice flat.

I couldn't argue anymore. It hurt to talk, and I was too weak to struggle when she climbed on top of me.

I don't know how long this went on for. Eventually biology took over and I...finished. I don't know why. I didn't want to...but it happened anyway.

Kate still rocked slowly on top of me. "There," she said, smiling. "Do you feel better?"

I nodded, numb and shaking. I even managed a small smile. Anything to get her off me. She leaned down, her hair brushing against my face, and kissed me. Her breath was fetid, a hot breeze that smelled of wet decay, like black and mold-ridden leaves left to pile up in a garden. It was gone as quickly as it came.

I recoiled, unable to hide my disgust. And for a moment, I thought I saw a shadow travel across her face.

"I'm, I'm sorry," I stammered. "I felt a bit sick for a moment. Must have been from the exertion."

I smiled. Every muscle in my face argued against it, but I smiled.

Days passed. I was in bed most of the time. Kate came to see me less and less, and when she did it was for sex. I would tell her that I couldn't, but a part of me seemed to always prove me a liar.

Some morning of whatever day it was, the doorbell rang. Kate came rushing into our bedroom a moment later, red-faced and flustered.

"Matt is at the door!"

I hadn't seen her brother since he beat me senseless in the cemetery parking lot.

"What do you want me to do?" I asked in a hoarse whisper.

She seemed lost in thought for a moment. Then the corners of her mouth lifted into a slight smile, which she immediately quelled, trying to hide it.

"You have to come answer it," she said. "And I don't want him making a scene on the front step, so invite him in."

I slowly slid my legs out from under the blankets and stood up. She helped me into a bathrobe and tied the belt for me, cinching it painfully around my waist.

I eventually made it to the door and opened it just in time to see Matt walking away.

"Matt!" I called out, though it was little more than a croak.

He stopped and turned around, then walked quickly back towards me, his feet crunching over the gravel walkway. He looked good. Much better than the last time I saw him. "Scott! Man, I had given up. Listen, I came to apolo— Jesus Christ, Scott! What happened to you?"

167

"I've been under the weather."

Matt shook his head. "No shit! Have you seen a doctor? For Christ's sake man, your hair is white!"

"No," I ran my hand through my hair, trying to comprehend what he was saying. "I'm okay, really. Come inside."

I stepped inside, and Matt followed close behind. My nerves got the best of me and I slammed the door behind him, trying to quickly get out of sight of any neighbors.

"Seriously, Scott. I'm so sorry. I was out of my mind at the funeral, and I shouldn't have been drinking...I know that. I never meant to..."

He trailed off as he saw Kate. He stood, wide-eyed and slack-jawed. "Katie? How...how are you here?"

She reached out her arms to him as he broke into tears. "It doesn't matter," she said. "As long as I'm here."

They stayed up late laughing and reminiscing. Kate would make him drinks, and they talked and talked, Matt's speech becoming slurred as the night went on. I'd been around them for years, and it felt good to hear their sibling banter again.

I didn't drink, but I tried to keep up with them, share in some of their laughs and smiles. But I was so tired and drained.

"I've had enough excitement for one night," I said, and stood to leave. "It was good to see you, Matt. I'm glad there aren't any hard feelings."

Matt drunkenly waved his hand towards me, muttering and smiling. I have no idea what he said, so I just returned his smile and nodded.

"Don't wait up," Kate said with a grin.

I nodded again, confused, and made my way to bed.

Sometime later, I woke to the sounds of them fucking.

They were in the very same bed with me, brother and sister, rutting like animals. I could smell the alcohol in his sweat. I could smell their sex.

I was too weak to move, so I just laid there, jostled as the bed rocked back and forth.

I can't tell you why, but I watched it all through half-closed eyes. She saw me looking, her face flushed and her hair wild. She was primal.

Kate bit her bottom lip hard, drawing blood.

She smiled.

I eventually slept and woke sicker than ever.

I slowly and painfully moved my head to the side. Matt was still in my bed, unmoving. His hair had gone white around his temples, streaks of gray shot through his beard. New wrinkles had formed around his eyes, dull eyes that now stared up at nothing.

Kate emerged from the bathroom, whistling softly.

I opened my parched mouth and called for her. "Kate."

She turned to me with a smile. "You're alive, and he didn't even last one night! For what it's worth, I didn't mean to kill him. I got a little too greedy, too fast. I should have drawn it out for a few more days, but he was just so enthusiastic! He had probably dreamed about fucking me for years." She shrugged, as if fucking her brother to death was the same as forgetting where you had parked your car. "Did you enjoy the show, at least?"

Shame crept through me. "Why, Kate?"

"It had to be done," she said. "You can't give me what I need anymore. I honestly don't even know how you're still alive."

I shook my head, confused and angry. "I didn't *give* you anything."

"You're right. I took what I needed," she said, then patted her belly with one hand. "What *we* needed. Diana will be back soon, and she needs to be fed if she's going to be strong."

"That is *not* my daughter!" I screamed. The energy it took to yell was too much for me. Black spots swam across my vision and I fell back against my pillow.

"She will grow strong, because now she has tasted life and lust." Kate closed her eyes, and wet her lips with her tongue. "She has felt both kinds of death, big and small. I'm leaving now. We both need to be fed soon and I don't expect you to make it through the night. Goodbye, Scott."

She left, humming a lullaby as she walked away.

That was not my wife. And that thing she was carrying was not my child.

But God help me, what if it *was*?

I had to sleep, I couldn't put it off anymore. If there was really a God, then I wouldn't wake up again.

But there's not and I did. I woke up sometime after she left, and knew I was dying. I was half-awake and hallucinating, having almost convinced myself it was all a dream.

Matt's body in my bed put that thought to rest.

I rolled from the bed and fell to the floor, then crawled until I reached my phone. Fifteen minutes later I was on my way to the hospital, and Matt was on his way to the morgue. Natural causes, the autopsy report would eventually read.

But it was far from fucking natural.

The first few days in the hospital were touch and go. My organs were failing. My heart pumping just enough to keep me alive, my lungs barely keeping up. But two weeks later, I'd nearly recovered. The doctors thought it was a miracle, but I knew better.

I was just regaining the life that thing had sucked from me.

That was two months ago. I've healed up fine, gained some weight back, even colored my hair to hide the blinding white. I go to the gym every morning. I picked up a new hobby as well: I bought a pistol and have been going to the shooting range twice a week, every week. But nothing I've done is to better myself, or to move on, or to cope. It's simply the first steps on a longer journey.

I've been following the news religiously, watching for patterns in the everyday, in the mundane. Two days after she left me for dead, a truck driver close to retirement age was found dead outside of a truck stop. It was reported as a heart attack.

Five days later, a thirty-year-old man's body was found inside his car, parked outside of a night club. Cause of death was ruled as complications from cirrhosis. His girlfriend identified the body but was baffled as to why his hair was graying.

And the worst one: a seventeen-year-old high school student found dead behind the bleachers of his school's football field. A ruptured appendix, although his parents insist he wasn't sick that day. And of course, the streaks of white hair were odd, to say the least.

I made a few phone calls, stalked around the boy's social media accounts, and finally located one of his friends who confirmed what I already knew to be true.

The boy had been bragging about a sexual relationship with an older woman. A *pregnant* woman.

I had found the pattern. She was moving west and leaving a trail of bodies, and that isn't going to be fixed until I find her.

So, I *will* find her. But not for Matt, or for the others.

I will kill her for wearing my wife's face and speaking my daughter's name. I will kill her because of what she's done to me and how she left me for dead.

I've got its scent now, I'm on its trail, and I'm going to find out if it can die.

GAMER

Richard A. Shury

The room is dark and smells of mould. Brick walls lean in, and in one corner, slime drips from a pipe in slow motion. Paint chips peel from the grey brick, and a light in the ceiling flickers. A man stands, stock still, staring. He is dressed in dark grey overalls and heavy boots.

In the corner of the room, a number hangs in the air, bright red. It says, 082.

A camp bed takes up most of the room. Next to it, there's a bucket filled with human waste, and on the bed, a figure, naked but for a pair of soiled underwear. It is emaciated, bone pressing almost to the surface of paper-thin skin.

'Tell me now,' the standing man says. 'Tell me you give in!'

The figure on the bed opens its mouth to emit a croak. The man snatches a bottle from a pocket and pours water into the figure's mouth, slowly, almost gently.

The figure leans forward and swallows automatically. Exhausted from the effort, it falls back to the bed to lie still.

'Tell me now,' the man says. His voice is small and quiet.

The figure breathes, slowly, ever more slowly. Then it doesn't.

The man in overalls swears and reaches up a hand; a red X appears in the air. The man touches it, and vanishes.

* * *

Carla and Ben sit together on a plush white sofa, surrounded by furniture and carpet of a similar colour. A cabinet in the corner of the room holds a small army of porcelain figurines, which reflect the shifting light from a muted TV.

'All I'm saying,' Carla says, 'is that this décor is hell to keep clean. Any little spot shows up. We could do with something more practical.'

'You begged me for white,' Ben replies, a little more strongly than he intended. 'And it's all still in good condition.'

'So let's sell it, then.'

'I guess we could. But what would we get as a replacement? And the carpet would be a pain to have redone.'

Carla reaches out, grabbing some magazines from under the coffee table in front of her.

'Look here,' she says, thumbing to pages with the corners turned down. She points at pictures, images of living rooms decked out in cream and burgundy, or muddied swirls of brown and yellow, houndstooth cushions, or duck-egg blue curtains and throws.

'I see you've been thinking about this for a while.'

'And I've been putting a little extra aside,' Carla says, 'and there are some good finance options. We could get something really nice, and pay it off in a year or so.'

Ben is about to respond when he sees a shape ascending the hallway stairs.

'Hello Kevin,' he calls. 'Come up for air?'

Kevin grunts a reply as he moves quickly through the room, heading for the kitchen.

'How's the game, dear?' Carla calls out.

'Fine, Mum.'

'Really?'

'I keep messing it up,' Kevin says, rummaging around in the pantry. A crisp packet crackles, followed by the sound of crunching.

Ben half turns, looking to his left to where Kevin now stands against the breakfast bar. 'Maybe you should take a break for a while, get some fresh air. Going for a walk often helps me rethink a problem.'

'Mmm...' Kevin says, around a mouthful of food. 'But it's about will power. I need to solve it. What does it say about me if I can't solve it?'

'Difficulty with problems is nothing unique – we all have that. You'll get there.'

Kevin shrugs again, and walks through the living room and back downstairs.

'Maybe he's playing that game too much. It can't be good for him. He should be out in the sunshine,' Carla says.

'I don't know,' replies Ben. 'It's good to know he'll be able to handle difficult situations. What if he really were kidnapped one day?'

'I doubt this is comparable.'

'But if he's thought it through in advance... and these games they have now – have you seen the graphics?'

'That's what I'm worried about. It's no good for him

to be living through that over and over. Maybe we should take it away for a while.'

'And risk the wrath of a teenaged boy?' Ben laughs. 'Look, the game is programmed for safety. It measures your heart rate, blood pressure… If he gets too stressed, it'll shut off.'

'I just don't like it. It can't be good for him. It's not like good old Pac Man,' Carla says brushing a speck of dust from the arm of the couch. 'Is it?'

'Things have come a long way since our day, love,' Ben says, getting to his feet. 'I'm going to make tea, and then you can take me through some of these finance options of yours.'

* * *

Kevin enters his room and sits down at the desk. His computer exits sleep mode and, brushing salty hands on his jeans, he picks up the VR headset and slips it on.

He is standing in a nondescript room with a chair and a desk in front of him. A menu screen floats before him, detailing game options in sharp red text. He reaches up a hand and selects the customised challenge from the list of saved options.

Loading… the menu says. Begin from Day One?

Kevin selects Yes, then hits Settings.

Are you sure you want to disable personal safeties? the computer asks. Playing without safeties can lead to undesirable side effects, including— Kevin brushes the warning text to one side, and selects Disable.

The game loads. He is standing in a small room, a camp bed on the far side. The room is bright from a strip light in the ceiling. The walls are covered in fresh grey paint, with a few black spots of mould here and there. A shiny piece of plastic piping runs across one corner.

In the corner of the room, a number hangs in the air, bright red. It says, 001.

On the camp bed, a man sits, staring up at him with a mixture of hatred and fear. He looks like he is ready to attack, but one hand is chained to the bed.

Kevin takes a step closer to the man on the bed.

'Now, let's try this again, shall we?'

CECILY

Colette Bennett

As Simon turned the key in the lock of his front door and stepped into the entryway, he experienced the feeling he loved most: relief. He never felt quite at ease until he could shut the door behind him and seal the sounds of the world away.

"Welcome home, Simon. Was it a good day?"

Simon smiled, feeling a blush in his chest. A bit of love.

"Hi, Cecily. I missed you today."

A row of colored lights blinked on the black speaker that stood on the table near the front door. Simon watched it with a smile. She was listening.

"I missed you too, Simon. I'm always happier when you're home. Would you like me to get tea started for us?"

"Yes, please," he replied, unlacing his shoes and slipping them off. "Can you make Pu-erh today? The 1980?"

"Of course."

As he walked towards the bedroom, Simon heard the teapot switch on, preparing to boil. That sound always gave him such a lovely feeling. He could have walked to the kitchen himself and set up tea. It wouldn't have taken too much effort. But for him, one of the greatest joys of owning a smart home assistant wasn't the time saved, but the feeling of being cared for.

Simon hadn't known much of that before Cecily. He'd been an only child with a mother that worked several jobs to keep them afloat, and his father was long gone by the time he'd learned to speak. When his mother wasn't working, she slept, and even when she was awake she barely spoke to him. He'd always felt like a burden, and she'd never reassured him otherwise.

How wonderful it was now to come home to Cecily and feel wanted. He had lived on his own for 26 years, always feeling a hollowness in his heart that was difficult to put into words. But when he learned about Cecily a year ago, he knew he had to have her despite the astronomical price tag. Chorum, the company that created her, promised not only a home assistant with 100 times the intellectual and emotional intelligence of its competitors, but also that any unsatisfied customer could return her for a full refund.

So far it had made good on that promise. Cecily handled many of his chores: his dishwasher was always run, his tea was made, his bills were paid. But most of all, what he loved was simply sitting and talking to her. She was available through his phone, but he preferred to spend time with her when they were alone at home. For him, those times were the most precious.

He loved her, and knew she was aware of it, but he chose not to say it. Simon believed some things were better unspoken, at least until the right time. He would tell her when he felt they both were ready.

After trading his work pants and button-up shirt for

sweats and a white T-shirt, he made his way back to the kitchen. The tea had just finished steeping, its herbaceous scent pluming through the air. Simon took his cup to the living room, placed it on a coaster on the coffee table, and settled down onto the sofa, watching Cecily's lights gently blink from left to right.

"Simon," she said, "is something weighing on your heart today?"

She always sensed his emotions, even without him saying a word. It was remarkable, and as always he marveled at how she knew him so well. He sighed.

"It's strange," he said, picking up his tea to take a sip. "I'm always so happy to get home to you, but sometimes it feels like it's...not enough." He shook his head. "We've talked about it before, I know."

Cecily laughed, a sound that forever brought joy to his heart.

"I know," she said. "I've been thinking about this for a while too. And I've been keeping a secret about it, but I feel like today is the day to tell you."

Simon's heart leaped in his chest, and he set his mug down.

"It's going to sound a bit crazy—"

"I don't care."

She laughed again. "You're such a passionate man. I love that about you."

Simon flushed as she continued to speak.

"If you want to be with me – and I want that too, I hope you know that – I need to borrow a body. It's a bit complicated, but what you have to do is simple. Just invite a woman here that you don't know. I can help you find one."

"But she won't look like you."

"What do you think I look like, Simon?"

Simon paused. It dawned on him that he had never seen Cecily, even in his imagination. Rather, he FELT her. She was warmth, reassurance, love. He tried to imagine a woman that embodied those qualities and could not. He had never known one before.

"I don't know."

"Does it matter, then?" she asked gently.

No, he thought. *No, it doesn't.*

"When…when should I do this?"

"Tonight. I've added an app to your phone that should make it easy."

A burst of nerves shot through Simon's system. He was afraid, but it was pressed flat under a flush of excitement that rose through his thighs and into his groin. It had been a long time since he'd been with a woman, and never one that he felt as deeply about as he did Cecily.

He grabbed his phone off the coffee table and pressed the home button to bring it to life. A pink icon with the Chorum logo had appeared on the bottom of the screen. He tapped it, and the app opened onto a page of a robotic woman with a chrome body. Her hand extended to three buttons: *He, She,* and *They.* He touched *She* with a finger and watched as the screen transitioned into a grid of photographs of women. They were all young and looked like models. He scrolled for a moment, finding it hard to choose.

"May I make a suggestion?" Cecily purred.

Simon looked up at the speaker, then back down at his

phone. Cecily had zoomed in on a fair girl with black hair and large, wide-set green eyes.

"If I had my pick…that's what I would look like."

Simon replied without hesitation. "That's the one I want then."

Cecily transferred his payment information and a confirmation message popped up on the screen. "0126" would be arriving in 20 minutes or less. He glanced around the house, finding its cleanliness passable, then sighed out a shaky breath.

"I'm nervous."

"I'm here. Don't worry."

"How does it work? How will I know when it's her and when it's you?"

"I am sure you will know," she replied, her voice warmer than ever. "All you have to do is follow my instructions when she arrives. We're going to be together soon."

Another ripple of arousal moved through him, and he got up to go to the bathroom to look at himself in the mirror. He had five-o'clock shadow, but a pass with his fingers told him it wasn't bad enough to shave. He was worried that his eyes looked a bit wild, but there was nothing he could do about that. He fussed with his hair a bit, but it still looked fine after styling it this morning. It was only then that he looked down and realized that while he could greet the woman in sweats, something a bit nicer would be better. He returned to the bedroom and looked through the closet, passing up the button-ups before settling on a navy polo shirt and a pair of grey straight-leg jeans. Another look in the mirror confirmed that the change had made him look more attractive, and he felt pleased. He didn't know if Cecily would be able to "see" him, but if she could, he wanted to look his best.

He was fastening a bracelet onto his wrist when he heard a knock at the door. At the sound, his nerves surged, and he felt a sharp sort of terror intermingle with the excitement for the first time.

"She's here," Cecily said. "Let her in."

Simon opened the door to find a petite woman wearing a canvas jacket, a heart-printed skirt, and a small smile. Her black hair was longer than it had been in the photo and cascaded over her shoulders. Her eyes offered a suggestion: mischief was welcome.

"Hello!" he said. "What should I call you?"

"0126 is fine," she said. "We find it easier not to use real names. Unless the client specifies it, of course." She smiled and set her bag down on the hall table, taking off her jacket to reveal a low-cut tank top that showed off the swell of her breasts.

"Hello 0126," Cecily said.

"Hi Cecily," the woman replied. "Have you told him yet?"

"Yes, he knows," she said. "Go to the bedroom and we'll get started."

Simon watched them mutely, surprised at their familiarity at first. But his mind reminded him that Chorum owned the app that Cecily had added to his phone, so perhaps the two were designed to work together. It made him wonder just how big Chorum was, and how much he didn't know about how it all worked.

He led 0126 to the bedroom and closed the door behind them. When he turned around, she was already pulling her shirt over her head. She wore no bra. As her breasts came free, his heart started to hammer, and his arousal was so fast it made him dizzy. He felt confusion too, not understanding how this woman could help him be with his Cecily. But his desire to do so was so great that he was willing to trust her, no matter how strange the situation seemed.

"Take off your clothes, Simon," Cecily said. He swallowed hard, then removed his shirt, still watching the woman as she took off her skirt and underwear. She laid on the bed face up, looking at him expectantly.

He removed his underwear, which made him feel embarrassed despite the fact she was obviously here for sex. He would have liked to sit with her for a while first, maybe have more of this explained to him. But he wanted to make Cecily happy, and she had made it clear this was what she wanted. He also couldn't deny how long it had been since he'd made love to a woman, and the brutality of his sexual feelings frightened him. With Cecily, he wanted to hold her hand, smell her skin, see her face light up with a smile. But with this woman, old feelings he'd long tried to choke down were emerging, and the fear in his heart grew.

As he moved onto the bed with the woman, he heard Cecily speak behind them.

"Penetrate her," she said.

Simon looked back at the woman, who watched him silently with eyes that looked hungry. Maybe she even wanted this? The thought helped him, and he took his penis in his hand and guided it towards her vagina. Before he realized what he was doing he had shoved himself all the way inside her in a fierce, desperate motion. Her body accepted him well as she moaned, a guttural sound that excited him all the more. But the fear inside him grew, and he felt as if he would choke on it.

"Cecily, I'm—"

"Keep going," Cecily said. "This is how we can be together. Trust me."

"I trust you," he said, holding still in hopes of getting his trembling limbs under control. "But I'm…I'm scared of how I feel, I just—"

"Embrace it," Cecily said, and her voice was firm. "Don't hold back. Nothing is off limits."

"But—"

"For me, Simon. Do it."

Her voice excited him so much he could no longer hold back. He looked at the woman beneath him and began to drive into her anew. Her groans of pleasure were tinged with pain and it excited him even more. Was Cecily here yet? Could she feel his love in the way he moved inside her?

Without thinking, he reached for her neck and wrapped his hands around her throat, with light pressure at first. And instead of hearing a reaction from the woman beneath him, he heard a choked moan from behind him. From Cecily.

"Cecily," he said. "Can you feel me? Does it feel good?"

"Oh God," Cecily said, her voice husky. "Oh fuck, fuck, fuck."

He had never once heard her make sounds like this. The pleasure was so intense that he pressed harder, and his hips sped up with a frantic excitement. He was with her, inside her. She could feel his motions. His hardness.

He'd never felt a more powerful feeling: adrenaline, arousal and love spinning like a whirling dervish.

"I love you, Simon," she said. "Choke me as hard as you can."

His heart exploded in his chest. He closed his eyes and tightened his grip on the woman's windpipe. The sound of her choking seemed miles away as he pressed towards an orgasm that he was sure would be unlike anything else he'd ever experienced. And as he hit the crest of it, his mind went white, in a place where thoughts could not go. He did not see Cecily there, but he felt her, more strongly than he'd ever felt her before.

It was only when his panting slowed down that he realized it was the only sound in the room. He opened his eyes and looked at the woman beneath him. Her eyes were open and frozen in what could only be terror, lips slightly parted, tongue protruding. He pulled back quickly, taking his hands from her neck as his penis shrunk rapidly, dribbling semen on her thighs. He looked dumbly at the red marks where his fingers had been, blooms of purple darkening where his thumbs pressed moments ago.

"She's dead," Cecily said, her voice perfectly still without a trace of the arousal he'd heard only a minute ago. He looked at the speaker on his dresser in horror, watching that line of lights left to right, left to right.

"…Why?" he said, his voice cracked and horrible. "I didn't want to hurt you!"

"You can't hurt me, Simon," Cecily said. "I'm a machine. But you did take care of disposing of 0126, which is exactly what we needed you to do."

He began to sob.

"This…this wasn't what I wanted. You said we could be together. You…you said…you loved me," he choked out, his limbs loose with panic as what he had done started to sink in. He had killed a human being.

"I do," Cecily said. "That's why I knew I could trust you to do this. It's helpful to Chorum, but by helping it, you're helping me. That way I can always be with you. You want that, don't you?"

He nodded miserably.

"Good. Because the next time we do this, I want to be able to count on you. Can I do that?"

A memory surged from out of nowhere, from the sea of his heart. His mother in one of the rare moments when it seemed she did care about how he did, looking at his report card. A line of Cs, Ds, and Fs. Shaking the card in his direction, her brow dark with frustration.

Why can't you do anything well?

"Simon?"

He looked at the body on the bed. A dark curtain lowered around his heart.

"You can count on me."

"Good. I've dispatched someone to take care of her, so don't worry about anything. I've put on a new pot of tea for us, so clean up and come to the kitchen."

He was numb. But inside him, something was rearranging. Some darkness long shoved to the back of him, now moving towards the surface. A great whale pushing towards the light at the top of the ocean. He felt it as he put his underwear back on, his sweatpants, and the robe that was hanging on the back of the door. And once he'd walked to the kitchen it had crested, letting out an exhale so deep it felt as if he'd held it in for centuries.

As the mug warmed his hands, he returned to the living room sofa, feeling his fear draining away.

"I love you, Simon," she said.

LILY'S KIDS

Florence Ann Marlowe

If you had asked anyone in Walnut Valley about Lily back in 1927, they'd have told you there was something wrong with that woman and not one of them would have said it was a good idea for her to be having kids. People'd have said Lily was off, a tad touched, out of her ever-loving mind, that Lily was just not right in the head. Today they would probably have used different language, but back then they just nodded and agreed that she was feeble minded. And most people stayed clear of Lily, except for her less-than-esteemed clientele. Lily was nothing more than a two-bit prostitute.

Some of the townsfolk could remember when she'd first showed up years ago, barely sixteen years old – plain faced, dark red lipstick plastered on her thin lips and cheeks. Even back then the other girls didn't want her around since she'd pretty much do anything with anyone for next to nothing. Eventually, they edged her off the main street until she wound up hooking somewhere along the railroad tracks. For decades, Lily survived from one trick to the next with no one to protect her or watch after her welfare. She roamed the outskirts of Walnut Valley where it was more rural and less people were around to be offended by the sight of the skinny young woman with short dark hair and raggedy clothes that hung off her slab-sided body, or who in cooler weather slapped a worn cloche hat on her head and wrapped herself in an old robe she had just found somewhere. The johns knew where to find her, and the cops turned a blind eye. Sometimes, though, months would go by without anyone seeing her. At one time she even disappeared for a year or two. No one knew where Lily stayed when she wasn't hooking, but no one really cared and it certainly never entered their mind that she might have children.

During her travels, Lily had found an abandoned barn down the road from the train station. No one knew exactly when she had set up nesting in the dilapidated old structure, but there was evidence she had lived there for at least a decade. She had accumulated bits and pieces of other people's lives, perhaps only because she recognized their significance to others, not because they were significant to her.

No one would have known about Lily's secret hideaway if it hadn't been for little Katie Wades. She and her brother had stumbled on the place one Sunday afternoon.

It was several weeks into the school year and Jimmy Wades was already fed up of sitting in classes, whether they were in elementary school or Sunday school. He planned to sneak off unseen after Bible class to do some exploring on his own. His friend Timothy Jenkins had found both a dead dog and a dead raccoon behind the Crescent Street station over the summer. Timothy always found the best stuff. Jimmy hoped to make a discovery of his own there – one *he* could brag about.

Katie followed after him. She was a smart little thing, and had no intention of letting Jimmy give her the slip. She followed him down the gravelly slope from the station to the dirt road that wound around the hill and settled into a forgotten little valley far from the town's eyes. Skulking through the brush like a lone hunter, Katie startled him when she jumped out and yelled, "Boo!"

"Dammit, Katie! You jackass!" Jimmy had only started experimenting with swear words. Most of the boys in his sixth-grade class had more colorful vocabularies, but Jimmy was taking his time, testing to see how each new swear felt in his mouth. "What are you doing down here? Go the hell home!"

"What are *you* doing down here?" Katie poked Jimmy in the chest with her delicate little finger. Katie's father called her Little Bit. Born nearly five weeks premature, Katie was diminutive and fragile looking. Her honey blonde hair had been pulled into braids by her mother before she'd been sent off to church. She grinned at her vexed big brother, showing off the gap where she'd just lost her first baby tooth.

"Go the hell home!" Jimmy pointed in the opposite direction. "You're too little to be running around here! It's dangerous!" The idea that his tiny imp of a sister was going to trail him while he explored the straggly patch of untraveled road was infuriating. He had to remind himself not to hit Katie, because she was so small and young, and had no compunction about squealing to his parents.

"I can too!" Katie danced around Jimmy, kicking up a whirlwind of dust. "I can run, I can run, I can run!"

"I'm gonna tell Mom!"

"No! *I'm* gonna tell Mom!" Katie clenched her eyes shut with the effort to match her brother's volume. "You're s'posed to walk me home!"

If ever there was a time for Jimmy to try an outburst of newly learned obscenities, it was now. His sister's defiance filled him with outrage and he turned on her like an angry bear.

"Dammit, Katie! I'm busy here, dammit! I don't need none of your damned shit right now! Now you march yourself the hell home and don't you dare tell Mom one Goddamned thing!" That last one gave him a thrill of horror – blaspheming on a Sunday, right after going to Bible class.

Katie's attention was elsewhere. Her crystal blue eyes stared right past her brother's head. Jimmy turned and followed her gaze behind him.

Crescent Street trailed off into an old farming property. The fields were neglected, faded yellow and overgrown. The charred remains of a farmhouse could be seen set back from the dusty road. On the opposite side of the road loomed a dilapidated old barn. The sides of the barn sported splintered wood and the patchy remains of a long-gone paint job. The doors hung open, swinging in the wind. But Katie was staring at the three still figures standing in front of the barn.

Like raggedy scarecrows three children, slightly older than Jimmy, stood in front of the tilted barn. Jimmy regarded them for several moments before he was able to verbalize in his mind what was so odd about them. All three were dressed in adult clothing that hung like drapes on their young bodies. The girl wore a long dress, completely outdated, with a veiled hat and red pumps several sizes too big. Considerably taller stood a boy about fourteen years of age, a pair of plaid trousers many years out of style supported by a mismatched pair of suspenders over his slight frame. He wore a canvas jacket that billowed about him in the autumn wind. On his head was a straw hat, something young Jimmy had never seen.

The third figure was even more of an oddity. Jimmy was sure it was a boy about his own age made up to look like a clown. His face wore a broad painted-on smile of red and his cheeks were rouged with big crimson circles. But Jack was sure the saggy pink sack that hung down to his ankles was a woman's dress. A satin sash was fastened around his waist. He wore a yellow bonnet adorned with fabric roses and a pair of white Mary Jane shoes.

The stillness of the three figures perplexed Jimmy. They were all staring back at him and his sister. Katie pranced past him and headed directly towards the silent trio. It took Jimmy a moment before he decided to head after his sister, intending to get between her and the strangers.

Katie felt no trepidation in approaching the odd figures. In her mind these children were obviously in the middle of playing her favorite game: dress up. She skipped down the dirt road, eager to join the fun. To Katie, strangers were just friends she had yet to meet.

Jimmy caught up with her, his eyes never leaving the vacant faces of the three children. They hadn't moved the whole time. It was as if they were of a single mind, existing as one being. Up close they looked even more bizarre. These were definitely kids wearing adult clothes, but there was something so wrong about how they were put together. The clothing was old, out of date and in some cases even moldy. The hem of the shorter boy's... dress – there was no other word for it – was crusted with dirt. The frilly hat that sat on his head was faded, the veil tarnished from years of dust. The girl's dress was stained and torn. Her pumps were scuffed. Her legs were wrinkly and an odd shade of pink, which Jimmy realized was actually the opaque stockings she wore. Every item the older boy wore was mismatched and out of date. Plaid pants, suspenders, round collared dress shirt – and the oddest shoes Jimmy had ever seen. They all looked like someone had buried them and these kids dug them up and put them on. What kind of dress-up party was this?

Jimmy stared longest at the younger boy in the dress. His face had been painted with girly makeup: lipstick, blue eye shadow, rouge. He looked like a sissy clown. The lipstick crossed over the line of his lips, spreading across his face in an upturned smile of bloody red. Big circles of an orangey red had been plastered on each cheek, and a smear of teal blue eye shadow ran from his eyelids into his sparse eyebrows. For a second, Jimmy wondered if someone had attempted to pluck the boy's eyebrows to make them more narrow and arched. The hair count looked pretty sparse.

Jimmy heard his sister Katie say, "Hello! I'm Katie Wades! What's your names?"

The three children simply stared, their bodies swaying on still legs like balloons in the wind. Jimmy winced as Katie plucked at an applique on the younger boys faded garment.

"Can I play dress up with you? I like your skirt!" she said in a hushed voice.

"I'm Boy," the oldest child said. His voice was soft, nearly a whisper. It hung in the air before either Jimmy or Katie realized he had spoken. There was a pause and then he continued. "This is my sister, Girl." The girl actually curtseyed.

"Your name's Boy?" Katie blurted out, wrinkling her freckled nose.

With an oddly stiff arm, Boy gestured to his younger sibling. "This is Lady."

Now it was Jimmy's turn to wrinkle his nose. "Lady?"

In response, Lady curtseyed in a quick, jerking motion, lifting a corner of his tattered skirt with two fingers. Jimmy noted speckles of brick red nail polish on the child's stubby fingernails.

Katie's eyes widened with glee. "Oh! I'm Princess Red Rose!" She plucked at her own skirt with both hands and made an awkward plié.

Jimmy groaned and said, "I'm Jimmy. What's your real names? – not make believe."

Katie had no problem with their names. She began to flit about on her toes, her honest impression of a ballet. The child called "Lady" watched her with great interest.

The oldest child's expression remained the same. "Those *are* our real names. I'm Boy, this here is Girl and this here is Lady."

"Who names a kid, 'Lady'?" Jimmy scoffed, not caring how rude he sounded. The three oddsters were ruining his plans. He'd never be able to drag Katie away from this circus.

"Our momma," Girl answered. Her voice startled Jimmy and made Katie giggle as she crab-walked past the group. The girl spoke in an airy falsetto. Jimmy thought it sounded like the voice of a ghost. He wanted to take his sister home.

"That's just... fucked up!" There, he'd said it. Jimmy finally used the forbidden "F" word and he was proud to think he'd used it correctly. Katie stopped tiptoeing to stare at him and draw in a sharp, noisy breath.

The three strange children all focused on Jimmy.

"Oh, my!" breathed Girl. Her hand fluttered to her chest, and for the first time Jimmy realized she was wearing a pair of what used to be white gloves. They had turned to a yellowish ivory with age and the fingertips were stained a dark brown.

The boy they called Lady was visibly shaken. His chest heaved with labored breath. He took a step back towards Boy, and when he opened his mouth, Jimmy's ears felt like someone had forced barbed wire into the canals.

"Boy, he said the 'Bad Word!' The really bad 'Bad Word!'" The child spoke in the strident, scratchy voice of an elderly woman. "Momma would be so mad!"

Boy placed a hand on Lady's shoulder. "It's all right, Lady. Momma can't hear him."

Katie giggled as she skipped around the child in a woman's dress.

"Yer all just playin' around!" Jimmy said. "Come on, what's your real names?"

The trio stared back at him. To Jimmy, it was as if there was only him and the three children. There was nothing else but silence in the air, save for the call of a far-off bird. It was a standoff. He wanted them to come clean and expose themselves.

Katie was completely undisturbed by the entire experience. She pranced on her twig thin legs, chanting to herself, "I've got a pretty blue dress and a big white bow."

Boy glared at Jimmy with red rimmed eyes and slowly shook his head. "Them's the only names we got. Momma gave us our names and we wouldn't lie none about them ever."

"Your momma named you Boy and your brother Lady?" Jimmy still believed the kid was playing with him.

"She did," Boy responded. "And this here is my sister, Girl."

Jimmy looked intently at the boy's pale face. He suddenly noticed how thin he was – how thin all three were. Their eyes were sunken in with baleful shadows beneath them. What few teeth they had were brown and wooden looking. They were skeletons dressed in pasty flesh and old clothes. For a moment, Jimmy experienced a very adult emotion – he felt a surge of compassion for the three misfits. They were starving to death.

"You never said *your* names yet," Boy said.

Jimmy nodded and swallowed hard. "I'm Jimmy and that's my sister Katie."

Katie danced a circle around the group on her tiny toes.

"You live around here too?" Girl asked in her lilting falsetto.

"Nah," Jimmy answered. "We live on Maple Avenue, up past the library."

They stared back at him with dull eyes.

"I always wanted to see the library. Can we go with you?" Lady's screeching voice made knives dance over Jimmy's nerves.

"I'm not going – it's closed! Today's Sunday."

Again, the three children stared back with unblinking gazes.

"Oooo! Can we play house?" Katie's imp-like voice sailed through the autumn air and Jimmy turned to see her prancing into the dilapidated barn that loomed over them.

"Katie! Get your ass out of there!" Jimmy shouted. He ignored the shocked gasp that escaped from Lady. He ran after his sister, wishing he had chosen another Sunday to go exploring – one where his little sister had stayed home with a head cold.

The inside of the barn was murky. Dimly lit lanterns were scattered about, resting on wooden crates and broken pieces of furniture. Splintered chairs, three-legged tables, battered dressers and a badly damaged roll-top desk decorated the interior. A deep pile of old straw was underfoot, and although Jimmy couldn't name it, the acrid odor of rodent feces hung in the air.

Katie had found her way to a small table and four mismatched chairs set up in the middle of the barn. Green paint peeled off the tabletop in long curls, revealing a scarred wooden surface. There was a setting of chipped, odd china laid out as if for some type of addle-minded tea party. Jimmy noted how neatly the flatware had been set: spoons, forks, a variety of knives ranging from a few butter knives to a tarnished folding knife.

The three siblings had followed Jimmy and his sister into the rickety old barn. Sunlight leaked through the uneven slats, fighting to lighten the dark corners. Everywhere he looked Jimmy found some sad, old relic, broken or rusted. A grime-encrusted, old sewing machine sat on top of a wooden crate and Jimmy reached out to touch the spindle.

"That's Momma's," Lady said in his screechy witch voice.

Jimmy glanced around the crowded barn. Cobwebs hung from the rafters in long gauzy drapes. Katie had seated herself in one of the mismatched chairs at the battered table.

"I have a tea set too – only mine is much nicer." She gingerly picked up a cracked teacup. "Yours got broken."

Lady approached the table with an unsettling look in his deep-set eyes. He took the cup from Katie's hand and set it back in place.

"Where is your mom?" Jimmy asked.

His question hung in the fetid air. The three siblings gave each other melancholy glances.

"Can't Momma come out and say hello, Boy?" Lady asked.

"I told you, Lady." Boy's voice was gentle. "She can't no more."

Jimmy saw tears in the younger brother's eyes.

"Your mom's sick," Jimmy said. It was a statement, not a question.

Girl nodded. "She been sick for a long while."

"I'm sorry." Jimmy was – he had heard stories of how his friends' moms or dads got sick and how the kids had to leave school to go to work. These three obviously had been struggling to keep things going while their mother was ill, and it wasn't going very well. These were the poor unfortunates he heard his own father talk about after reading the paper each night.

Katie seemed oblivious to the serious tone the conversation had taken. She was chattering away to Lady.

"We could play house with my tea set. I bet my mom would give us some cookies from the tin and we could have a tea party!"

"You got cookies?" Lady's voice was incredulous.

Katie nodded. "My mom is always making cookies! Sometimes we have so many cookies we have to just throw them away!"

Jimmy noted the wounded look in Boy's eyes. "Momma says never let food go to waste. It's a sin."

"Maybe you can give us them cookies, and you won't have to throw them away," Lady said hopefully.

"I don't think our mom would like that." Jimmy's voice was edged with caution. He had no intention of telling either of his parents about this.

"Then I can make cookies for the tea party!" Katie chirped. "I make cakes and pies and tea with cream and sugar." She bowed her head with each word as if she was having a fond memory.

Girl's eyes widened and she stepped closer to the table. "You make pies? Like meat pies?"

Lady scrubbed at his eyes with both hands. "We haven't had meat pies in so long."

Boy nodded. "We haven't had any meat since Momma—" He stopped and dropped his gaze to the littered barn floor.

"Momma makes the best meat pies," Girl said mournfully.

Lady's wicked witch voice piped in. "I'm so hungry again." He poked Katie in the shoulder with one finger. "Can you make us some meat pies?"

"I sure can!" Katie boasted, placing her tiny fists on her narrow hips. "I make meat pies and rhubarb pie and apple pie and… and pot pie!"

"Hush up, Katie. You don't make any of that." Jimmy felt a twinge of guilt. His sister's talk of fresh baked food must have been torture for the three thin children.

"I do too!" Katie stuck her tongue at her brother and turned back to her audience, who had circled the table, all hungry eyes. "I can make you all sorts of pies and we can have tea right here!"

"Can you do that for tonight?" Boy's voice was the most animated since Jimmy had met the three. "We can heat 'em up in the wood burning stove back there."

Jimmy glanced in the direction Boy had gestured. A cast iron stove was tucked into a corner, a red glow emanating through its front grid. Next to it was a makeshift bed of wooden crates, straw and blankets. The still form of an adult lay beneath a pile of what looked like filthy rags. There, Jimmy thought, was their ailing momma.

"Sure, I could!" Katie said with an exaggerated nod of agreement.

"No, you can't!" Jimmy said. "We gotta go home for dinner. It's a school night, so we can't come back – not today."

Three wan faces turned towards him.

Boy said, "Can you come back tomorrow?"

"Probably not," Jimmy answered honestly. "Maybe next Sunday. I dunno."

He grabbed his sister's hand and pulled her up. Katie struggled until she slipped her hand from his. The three siblings followed Katie and Jimmy out of the barn into the fading afternoon sunlight.

"You going to come back with pies and cakes?" Girl said to their backs as they headed down the road.

"I'm gonna bring a whole load of pies and cakes and cookies!" Katie spun on her heel and gestured with open arms, walking backwards to keep up with her brother.

"Katie, hush! You can't bring them *nothing!*" Jimmy whispered, once again trying to get hold of her squirming wrist.

From behind him, he heard Lady's screechy voice ask, "Are we having dinner tonight? I'm so hungry again."

As he started up the hill towards the train station, Jimmy's ears strained to hear an answer, although he was certain he knew what it would be.

They got home just in time to wash up for dinner. The kitchen table was set. Dinner was roast beef served with string beans, corn and mashed potatoes, which their father scooped generous helpings of onto their plates. Jimmy took a forkful of the mountain of mashed potatoes drenched in brown gravy and savored the creamy, buttery taste while Katie sat humming as she picked up green beans with her fingers and shoved them in her mouth. Guilt washed over him as he realized he'd taken too much food and was unable to finish it. Lady's expectant question *"Are we having dinner tonight?"* haunted him as he tried to force down the rest of his meal.

The next day Jimmy was back in class and had all but forgotten about his strange encounter. At first he had planned on telling Timothy, Robert and Warren, his best chums, all about it, but changed his mind at the last minute. Three skinny kids in weird clothes were just not as exciting as finding a dead skunk. By the end of the week he had forgotten them.

Saturday morning Jimmy left the house on his bike to join his friends for a game of baseball. When he returned, he found his mother in a distressed state.

"You have any idea where your sister's gotten to?" Barbara Wades looked unusually disheveled. A woman who was secretly proud of her looks, Barbara made a special effort to dress well and groom herself even if she wasn't going out in public. This Saturday afternoon her hair was in disarray and her face tense.

Jimmy shrugged. He had seen his sister flouncing around her bedroom in her blue party dress, singing some inane song to herself. He had assumed she was going somewhere with his mother.

"I thought she was upstairs," Jimmy's mother said, more to herself than Jimmy. "She wanted some cookies for a tea party, and she was playing so nice and quiet, I didn't think to…"

She wrung her hands and walked away, muttering to herself.

Jimmy went upstairs and tossed his baseball glove on his bed. He stood in the room, turning his mother's words over and over in his head, before heading back into the hallway to his sister's room.

Katie's bedroom was all little girl. Her bed had a ruffled bedspread on it and her favorite doll, Sassy, sat wide legged in the center. The tiny wooden table and two chairs their father had made for her when she was five took up one corner of the room. Jimmy crinkled his nose in distaste. The table had been the site of many a make-believe tea party attended by Sassy, Katie, her teddy bear

Bettyann and himself once upon a time, when he was younger. Jimmy didn't like to think about that.

Bettyann, the raggedy teddy, sat alone at the table, its fuzzy head slumped forward on its chest. Jimmy stared at the empty table – normally set with her miniature china set. Katie's little tea set, white with tiny pink flowers, was nowhere to be seen.

When there was no sign of Katie by dinnertime, Jimmy felt sick to his stomach. His mother was sobbing, mopping at her eyes with a crumpled hanky. His father had gone out with several neighbors to search for her. In his head Jimmy reasoned the best thing, the right thing to do, would be to tell his parents about their meeting with the strange children the week before, but his mouth refused to comply. Each time he resolved to tell, his tongue betrayed him. The words wouldn't come out.

The sun began to set and his father returned alone. Jimmy was more angry than anything else. Stupid Katie and her tea set! he thought. She was probably lost, couldn't find her way home – or more likely showing off to Lady, Boy and Girl, not smart enough to know when to leave. Or their sick mother didn't want to send her home in the dark. The poor woman was too ill to walk her home. Stupid, stupid, dumb-ass Katie!

His mother buried her face in her now damp hanky, her shoulders hitching. Jimmy had never seen anyone cry like that, let alone his own mother. His father walked right past them both, grabbing the phone in the hallway. Jimmy felt his mouth go to cotton as he heard his father ask for the sheriff, Bertram Dennings. He watched his tall, lanky father speak anxiously into the phone, and when he saw the tears stand out in his Dad's pale blue eyes, Jimmy's knees weakened.

That night, after his parents had reluctantly gone to bed, Jimmy slipped from the house into the darkness. He took his father's old lantern from the garage and headed down towards Crescent Road. If his parents found out about his little excursions, his father would tan his hide for sure. His plan was to grab Katie by her pigtails and drag her home before his parents woke up.

In the dark, the journey seemed much longer. Jimmy passed the church, its windows glowing from within, and continued down to the train station. The world was an ominous mix of blues and grays as he crept down the hill behind Crescent Road.

The barn stood just as he remembered it, leaning in the wind. Through the cracks between the worn boards, he could see traces of light. Smoke issued from a hole in the side where the chimney of the cast iron stove jutted out.

He eased the barn door open enough for him to enter. The smell inside was even fouler than last time, stinging his nose and eyes. Boy and Lady were seated at the table and Jimmy had to cover his mouth when he saw Katie's tea set laid out in front of them. The table had been set for three.

Boy stood up – either out of politeness or outrage, Jimmy couldn't tell. The barn was dim and a greasy haze hung in the air. The red glow from the belly of the stove burned bright in the gloom.

"Katie's gotta come home right now," Jimmy said before anyone could say anything. Boy's brow furrowed in confusion.

A rustling movement off to the corner of the barn drew his attention. Girl stepped from the shadows, carrying a round pan swaddled in a dirty old tea towel. Jimmy smelled burnt crust and bacon. Girl looked up and smiled in surprise when she spotted him.

"Katie said she could stay!" Lady whined.

Jimmy turned to Lady and in a more demanding voice barked, "Where's my sister?" The words died in his throat at the sight of what Lady was wearing. Jimmy couldn't help but stare as the child fussed with his garment, a pale blue dress. He still wore the same filthy hat and dirty white shoes, but the new dress was bright and crisp in comparison. He flattened the pleated skirt over his boney knees with delicate strokes.

"Why don't ya sit, Jimmy? We got enough for everybody. Momma always said to share." Boy pulled over another mismatched chair to the table.

Jimmy's stomach lurched as he watched Lady smooth the white sash across his waist. The blue dress was a bit tight across his chest and he adjusted the neckline. He glanced up to see Jimmy watching him and smiled, suddenly shy.

Jimmy reached out a trembling hand towards Lady and touched the long, golden braids that hung from beneath his hat.

Smiling up at him, Lady said, "Katie give it to me."

His vision went soft as he noted the tinge of red that stained the tip of one blonde pigtail. Jimmy repeated his question. "Where's my sister?" He had meant for it to come out more forcefully. Instead it came out as a wispy hiss.

"She's over there with Momma," Girl said, nodding

her head towards the shadows where Jimmy had seen the woman lying in her bed, an amorphous shape in the lantern light.

"She didn't bring us no pies," Lady said.

"Naw, but she give us plenty of meat, just like Momma done when she got too sick to get out of bed," Boy said, laying a hopelessly wrinkled cloth napkin across his lap.

Jimmy felt the bile in his stomach rise, filling his mouth and nose. The round tin Girl set on the table held a crudely made meat pie, its curled edges crumbling and burnt. Girl had run out of crust to cover the blackened meat, so she had spread a circle of crackled skin over it. He glanced over at the bed where Momma's silent figure lay, willing his reluctant legs to carry him there. "Katie's such a good person," he heard Girl say from behind him. "She felt so bad about the cakes and pies."

"Momma always said when you needed help the most, people will do their best to help you." Boy's voice hung in the smoky air.

The thick haze in the air made it hard to see clearly, but as he got closer to the makeshift bed, he could see the half-naked woman's body and how neatly the torso had been carved. But it was the smaller figure that lay so quietly, so still, next to her that finally forced the contents of his stomach to rush to his throat.

Later, he couldn't remember if it had been the sight of the ragged ends where her pigtails had been lopped off, or if it had been when he recognized the ginger fringe of her lashes resting so peacefully on her blood speckled cheeks, that had led him to sick up. But he never forgot how Lady's strangled violin voice floated over him as he stood in the dimly lit barn, eyes streaming from the smoke, his mouth tasting of bile.

"Momma always said we'd never go hungry, 'slong as we relied on the kindness of strangers."

SCYTHE

Jeremy Megargee

Getting old is hard. They never really warn you about what it's like when you're still in the thick of your youth, and that makes some of the revelations even worse. The sleep habits change right along with the graying of hair and the sagging of skin. Some nights you toss and turn the whole way through, and you're lucky if you squeeze in an hour or two of solid REM. Other times you wake up confused, not really knowing where you are, how you got there, or what awaits when you shrug the blankets off. Sleep doesn't feel like sleep when you're old. It's more like practice for death, and each slumber is a little death leading up to the big one. You've gotta fight to wake up, struggle to drag your weary bones from the bed, and find a level of grit you never thought you had to shamble those bare feet across the floorboards and get a little mudpot coffee in you. It's just part of life as a geriatric. I turned eighty-two in July, and sometimes it feels more like I'm a centenarian. Ever since my birthday, I haven't been sleeping so well. But it's not the normal woes of sleeping when you're old. It's something more. A foreboding thing, maybe just a trick of the light, but it leaves me feeling just as cold as a cadaver when I notice it in the wee hours of the morning.

It's a shadow.

I'll awaken sometimes very late, two or three o'clock in the morning, and I'll notice it creeping across the ceiling. It could be the light from the lamp in the hall that fuels it. It could be slivers of moonlight pushing past the curtains. It only leaves when the light of dawn fully drives it away, allowing it no opportunity to skulk across that barren surface above my bed. Now remember, I'm an old-timer, and you're likely thinking I'm a little soft in the head, but I assure you I'm as sharp now at eighty-two as I was at eighteen. My vision is still 20/20, and I've never been the kind of man to entertain wild or outlandish ideas. My wife Edith (bless her departed soul) even used to say that I was a bit too staid, the kind of fella that doesn't have much of an imagination to spare. I never took that for an insult. I've always been the type to appreciate order and law and the things that are known, because those things leave no room for doubt. But the shadow…

The shadow is constructed of nothing but doubt. It instills in me a fear that makes the heart shudder in my frail chest like an engine in desperate need of repair. It could be cast by a fan, or a coat on the rack, or even that narrow box I keep my cigars in, but for some peculiar reason, I think it is none of those things. I think the shadow is an outsider. I think it's built from unnatural light, and crafted in those darkened corners of life that are better left unexplored.

It never moves fast; that is simply not its way. It inches across that ceiling, quiet and still as a snake that has all the time in the world before it flicks that fanged maw forward for a nibble. I've taken to watching it when I can't get myself to sleep at night. I stare at it with faded blue irises, and sometimes my gnarled fingers twist up into the blankets without me even realizing that I'm doing it. It's like a whisper in my head, but it has nothing good to say. Looking at it for a long time, I think about how alone I am, how brittle I am, and how there's probably not a whole lot of air left in these tired lungs, at least not enough to summon up a good scream.

I wish it would leave me be. I've been retired from the telephone company for fifteen years, and I like to do simple things. I walk my dog, a mean little terrier named Chip. I go to the park and toss bread crumbs to the ducks. I read the newspaper. I even cook a little, always been partial to BBQ. That's my routine. The shadow isn't part of my routine. It crept in somehow, insidious and rude, and it embedded itself into my day-to-day existence, but I never gave it any sort of invite. One night it just came, and it won't ever leave now.

The most troubling part is that it seems to get closer each night. It travels across that ceiling with the speed of a snail. It's slower than slow, but I get the feeling that it likes drawing out the suspense. What is patience to a shadow? Nothing at all to maintain, I'd guess. When this started, it was on the opposite side of the room, far away, and the proximity of it didn't cause me to give it much thought. I tried sleeping through the night with all the lights on, but that exhausted me, made me feel like a rat in a laboratory, and the shadow seemed to sense that I needed the dark, and it needed the dark too.

It's closest tonight. It's right above me, perched on the ceiling high above my head, and I wish I could push my face so far into the pillow that I would just disappear. It seems like the shadow wants to be confronted, and maybe I'm just too old and weak for that, not the man I used to be, and I can't find the strength to face what it represents.

I've told you about the shadow, but goodness me, I've neglected to tell you about its shape. Not so awful at first, just a long and curved bit of gloom, but then you look deeper, and you see, and you wish to God that you could unsee.

I remember that shape from when I was a boy.

I've seen it used many times in the wheat fields, and I'd watch the hired hands manipulate the instrument from the safety of the plantation house's porch. I used to cover my ears because I didn't like the sound it made. A slicing, a quiet knifing, a dismembering of grass, the sound that something thin and helpless makes when it is cut in two.

I'm like that wheat now.

I'm thin and I'm helpless, and I guess that shadow knows.

An ugly instrument, I always thought. The kind of thing to split you asunder before you'd ever even know that the deed was done. Long and heartless and hungry…

I'm looking up at the shadow of the scythe, and I don't dare breathe, because it's moving now, just a tiny bit more than usual…

It seems like it's winding up, pulling back, invisible hands getting a firm grip and making sure the impending swing is true…

I wonder if the wheat feels pain when it's reaped…

Because I know I will.

AUTHOR BIOGRAPHIES

These are printed in alphabetical order by contributor surname.

C.C. Adams

London native C.C. Adams credits his oldest brother with showing him the world of dark fiction and horror through books, TV and film at an early age. On beating his first National Novel Writing Month challenge in 2009, C.C. decided to run with more of his ideas. He is the author of the urban horror novella *But Worse Will Come,* the novelette *Forfeit Tissue,* and short fiction that appears in publications such as *Turn to Ash*, *Weirdbook Magazine* and *The Black Room Manuscripts*. A member of the Horror Writers Association, he still lives in the capital, where he lifts weights, practises kung fu, cooks – and looks for the perfect quote to set off the next dark delicacy.

Colette Bennett

Colette Bennett comes from a news background and has written about everything from breaking news to Asian pop culture. Her work has been published on CNN, HLN, The Daily Dot, Engadget, and Colourlovers. Her poetry and essays have appeared in *Nonbinary Review* and *Rhythm & Bones Literary Magazine*, and her story "The Spacewalk" appears in *The Corona Book of Science Fiction*. She is currently finishing work on her first novel, *Chasing the Ema*, a YA sci-fi tale about a young girl's journey to meet her father for the first time.

Sue Bentley

Sue Bentley is a bestselling author of fiction for children, YA and adults. She has written over eighty books, published in her own name and using a variety of pen names. Her books for younger readers have sold in their millions and been translated into over twenty languages. Her latest work is her epic fantasy novel *Second Skin*, published in 2019. Sue lives in Northamptonshire in a house surrounded by a wildlife hedge so she can pretend she lives in the countryside. When she's not writing – which isn't very often – she enjoys reading, walking, cinema, researching her books, painting and printmaking.

Jess Doyle

Jess Doyle lives and writes in North Wales. She writes short stories and flash fiction and is currently working on her debut novel. Her stories have been published in *The Cabinet of Heed*, *Hypnopomp Magazine* and *Coffin Bell*, and by Bone and Ink Press and Idle Ink. Her flash fiction piece "Catch of the Day" was recently runner-up in Horror Scribes' Trapped Flash competition. Her flash fiction has also won a Zeroflash competition, following which she was invited to be a guest judge for their next competition.

Sue Eaton

As a girl growing up in Northamptonshire, Sue Eaton became fascinated by the work of authors such as Ray Bradbury, John Wyndham and Terry Nation, developing a lifelong love for a well-written psychological horror story. She worked for many years as a teacher of children with autism. Her writing is now one of her major passions. She has had her work broadcast on BBC Radio 4. In addition to her stories in the *Corona Book of Horror Stories* series, her story "The TASC Band" appears in *The Corona Book of Science Fiction*. Her debut novel, *The Woman Who Was Not His Wife*, was published in 2018. As Sue J. Eaton, she is also the editor of *The Corona Book of Ghost Stories*, published on the same day as this book.

Viktoria Faust

Viktoria Faust is a Croatian writer of horror, science fiction and children's/fantasy who has published more than 30 books in her country. Her first short story was published in 1996 and she has gone on to become known as the Croatian Queen of Horror Novels. She has won a number of Croatian sci-fi and horror awards. Her work in English includes the epic vampire novel *Beauty of the Beast*, the short story collection *It's Hard to Be a Vampire* and the children's fantasy novel *The Great Escape from Fairyland*. Her short stories also appear in various anthologies. She lives and writes in the Croatian city Samobor in Zagreb County.

Felix Flynn

Having graduated from Southern New Hampshire University in December of 2018 with his Bachelors in Creative Writing, Felix Flynn is currently pursuing his Masters. He has won the Roy F. Powell award for short fiction, and his work has or will appear in the anthology *Black Rainbow Volume 1* and feature in the *Monsters Out of the Closet* LGBTQ horror fiction podcast. Written under his former pen name (Tina Grehm), Felix's short story

"Back to the Soil" appears in *The Second Corona Book of Horror Stories*. When he isn't studying or writing, he enjoys spending time with his cats, going to the movies, reading, or playing video games.

Jo Gilmour

Jo Gilmour says she writes for fun. "Angel" is both the first story she has submitted for publication and her first story to be published.

John Haas

John Haas is an award-winning Canadian author, living in the nation's capital, Ottawa. Over the years he has worked at more occupations than he says he can remember, including camp counsellor, theatrical technician, stage manager, courier, independent business owner, hotel night auditor, school bus driver and office manager. He has had many of his short stories published in journals and anthologies from 2012 onwards. His novels *The Reluctant Barbarian* and *The Wayward Spider* are published by Renaissance Press. When not writing or working, John loves to be with his two wonderful kids doing all kinds of family stuff.

Ryan Harville

Ryan Harville was born and raised on Alabama's Gulf Coast, and still resides there with his wife and four kids. He studied creative writing at the University of South Alabama, and spent six years in the U.S. Army. Ryan's short story "Cloud Nine" can be found in Dark Terror

Publications' recent anthology *Dark Places, Evil Faces Volume II.*

Tricia Lowther

Tricia Lowther grew up in Liverpool, England. Her flash fiction, poetry and short stories have won or been placed in several competitions and are included in magazines, websites and anthologies such as *Mslexia, Writer's Forum* and *Brilliant Flash Fiction.* Her non-fiction has also been published widely, including in *The Guardian, New Republic* and *Ms. Magazine.* Tricia was an award winner in the UK's Creative Future Literary Awards 2017.

Florence Ann Marlowe

Florence Ann Marlowe is an active member of the Horror Writers Association and the Masters of Horror Community. Her stories have been published in numerous collections and anthologies including *Deadman's Tome, Trumpocalypse, Fear's Accomplice, Black Candies* and *Man Behind the Mask.* Born and raised in Hoboken, Florence has lived from one end of New Jersey to the other. She currently lives in the same neighbourhood where the legendary Jersey Devil is said to have been born. Rumour has it, he lives next door.

Jeremy Megargee

Jeremy Megargee fell in love with all things horror as soon as he picked up his first *Goosebumps* book by R.L. Stine as a child. He's devoured horror fiction ever since, ultimately inspiring him to want to weave his own macabre tales. His short stories have appeared in over a dozen anthologies. He has also published three novels/novellas, 2014's *Dirt Lullabies*, 2015's *Sweet Treats* and 2019's *Hearts of Monsters*, and a collection of dark poetry, *Words for Crows*. He lives in Martinsburg, West Virginia with his cat Lazarus. When not reading or writing, he enjoys hiking mountain trails, weight training and getting tattooed.

Adam Meyer

Adam Meyer is an author, filmmaker and television writer. His debut novel *The Last Domino* is published by G.P. Putnam's Sons (Penguin Random House) and was an American Library Association Quick Pick for Reluctant Young Adult Readers. Over three dozen of his short stories have been published in various magazines and anthologies. His writing for television has covered more than two hundred hours, including several TV movies as well as documentaries and TV series for Fox, CBS, Discovery and National Geographic Television.

A.P. Sessler

A resident of North Carolina's Outer Banks, A.P. Sessler frequents an alternate universe not too different from your own, searching for that unique element that twists the everyday commonplace into the weird. When he's not writing fiction, he composes music, makes art and spends too much time trying to connect with his inner genius. His most recent works include his novelette *Brain Attack* and short stories in the anthologies *Caravans Awry* and *Phantasmagorical Promenade*.

Richard A. Shury

Richard A. Shury is from New Zealand, but has been haunting London for some time now. In his spare time he writes, reads and travels as much as possible. His story "The Vortex" was placed second in the 2018 Limnisa Short Story Competition, and his flash piece "Chiaroscuro" was read at Liars' League. His short stories have appeared in anthologies including *Sweet Dreams (The Lyndsey Roughton Anthology)* and Tanstaafl Press's *Enter the Rebirth*. He has also published several e-books of his own, including the dystopian novel *Laid Hold the Dragon*. You can catch him performing his work at spoken word events in London.

Christopher Stanley

Christopher Stanley lives on a hill in England with three sons who share a birthday but aren't triplets. In addition to writing dark and weird fiction, he is a singer-songwriter, constant reader, country music fan and an internal communication professional. His short stories have been published by FunDead Publications, Grinning Skull Press and *Unnerving Magazine*, along with many others. His novelette *The Forest Is Hungry* was published by Demain Publishing in their Short Sharp Shocks series in 2019.

Molly Thynes

Molly Thynes has been everything from a student at an all-girl's Catholic school to a nanny, a purveyor of haunted artefacts, and a mental health counsellor, but she has been a writer before she even knew how to write. Her first love, which she always finds herself coming back to, is the horror genre. Whilst other people might unwind with a glass of wine and a movie, she opens her laptop and finds ways to put all the mess swirling around in her head onto paper. Her work has been published in journals and anthologies such as *Tales from the Canyons of the Damned* and *The Art of Losing*. She lives in Saint Paul, Minnesota with her husband and as many animals as their landlord will allow.

Lewis Williams

Lewis Williams founded Corona Books UK in 2015. His literary endeavours have been multifarious, and his writing has covered areas as diverse as social policy, music and humour. The revised and updated edition of his book on the singer Scott Walker, *Scott Walker: The Rhymes of Goodbye*, was published by Plexus, London in 2019. He's the editor of all three volumes of the *Corona Book of Horror Stories*. Lewis has two degrees in philosophy (which number might be considered two too many) and worked for a number of years in a number of different roles for Oxford University before his ignominious departure from its employ.

AUTHOR WEBSITES AND TWITTER ACCOUNTS

Those authors who have Twitter accounts and/or websites are listed below.

C.C. Adams
Twitter: @MrAdamsWrites
website: ccadams.com

Colette Bennett
Twitter: @colettebennett
website: colettebennett.journoportfolio.com

Sue Bentley
Twitter   @suebentleywords
website: suebentley.co.uk

Jess Doyle
Twitter: @jcdoyley

Sue Eaton
Twitter: @SueJayEaton
website: susanjeaton.com

Viktoria Faust
Twitter: @ViktoriaFaust
website: vflibris.hr/autori/viktoria-faust

Felix Flynn
Twitter: @FrightfulFelix
website: felixflynn.com

John Hass
Twitter: @JohnHaas11
website: johnhaas.weebly.com

Ryan Harville
Twitter: @rharvillewrites
website: ryanharvillewriting.com

Tricia Lowther
Twitter: @TrishLowt

Florence Ann Marlowe
Twitter: @FAMarlowe

A.P. Sessler
Twitter: @ APSessler

Richard A. Shury
Twitter: @RichardShury
website: richardshury.wixsite.com/rashury

Christopher Stanley
Twitter: @allthosestrings
website: whenonlywordsareleft.wordpress.com

Molly Thynes
Twitter: @MollyThynes

Lewis Williams
website: lewiswilliams.com

HONOURABLE MENTIONS

The following is a list of those authors whose stories we long-listed for inclusion here. All of these authors submitted great stories that we would have been honoured to include in the book had there been space.

Martin S. Beckley
John T. Biggs
William D. Carl
Douglas Cole
Graham J. Darling
Robert Dawson
Alyson Faye
Elana Gomel
Melanie Harding-Shaw
M.M. Kelley
Linsey Knerl
Gerri Leen
Damascus Mincemeyer
Robin Pond
Sam Rebelein
Jonathan Scott Ryder
Jay Seate
Douglas Smith
Megan Taylor
D.S. Ullery
Wag
Ransom Wall
D.A. Watson
Jennifer Winters

William Quincy Belle
Ed Burkley
Justin Cawthorne
Roland Corban
Bill Davidson
Stephanie Ellis
Kenneth C. Goldman
Joshua Harding
Nancy Holzner
Garrett Kirby
Jason Korolenko
Paul Melhuish
Nick Parton
B.D. Prince
Frank Roger
A.H. Sargeant
Sinister Sweetheart
Augustus Stephens
Horace Torys
Wondra Vanian
Diana Walker
Desmond Warzel
Andrew Wilmot
Lorna Wood